DEIRDRE CASH (writing as Criena Rohan) was born in Melbourne in 1924 to Leo Cash, poet and entrepreneur, and Valerie Walsh, operetta principal. After her parents' divorce, a young Cash and her brother were cared for by relatives in South Australia and Melbourne. Cash began to write while boarding at the Convent of Mercy in Mornington. She later studied at the Conservatorium of Music.

Cash first married in 1948 and gave birth to a son, Michael Blackall, later that year. The marriage did not last, and Cash worked as a torch-singer and ballroom-dancing teacher to support herself. In 1953 she met the 'love of her life'—merchant seaman Otto Olsen. They married soon after, and their daughter Leonie was born the following year.

Cash's health started to deteriorate and she was hospitalised in Geraldton, Western Australia, with suspected tuberculosis. This four-month stay resulted in her first novel, *The Delinquents*. Rejected by several Australian publishers, *The Delinquents* was published in London in 1962, to acclaim. It was made into a cult film, starring Kylie Minogue, in 1989.

Eventually diagnosed with cancer, Cash wrote her second novel, *Down by the Dockside* (1963), while in and out of hospital, writing the last pages wearing an oxygen mask. Cash reportedly also completed a third novel, *The House with the Golden Door*, but no manuscript has ever been found.

Deirdre Cash died in Melbourne in 1963, aged thirty-eight.

NICK EARLS is the author of thirteen novels for adults and teenagers, three collections of short fiction and the Word Hunters series for children. Most of his books are set in or near Brisbane. Five of his novels have been adapted for theatre and two have become feature films.

ALSO BY CRIENA ROHAN

Down by the Dockside

The Delinquents
Criena Rohan

Text Publishing Melbourne Australia

textclassics.com.au
textpublishing.com.au

The Text Publishing Company
Swann House
22 William Street
Melbourne Victoria 3000
Australia

First published by Victor Gollancz Ltd, London 1962
This edition published by The Text Publishing Company 2014

Cover design by W. H. Chong
Page design by Text
Typeset by Midland Typesetting

Printed in Australia by Griffin Press, an Accredited ISO AS/NZS 14001:2004
Environmental Management System printer

Primary print ISBN: 9781922182142
Ebook ISBN: 9781925095142
Author: Rohan, Criena, 1924–1963.
Title: The delinquents / by Criena Rohan; introduced by Nick Earls.
Series: Text classics.
Dewey Number: A823.3

CONTENTS

Good Old, Sweet Old, Wholesome, Pure Little Brisbane
by Nick Earls

IN 1989, nearly thirty years after the publication of Criena Rohan's first novel, *The Delinquents*, Brisbane was on the cusp of change. Tony Fitzgerald had laid bare police corruption; an election was looming and the National Party was, for the first time in a generation, doomed to lose office. Meanwhile, at the Park Royal Hotel, my girlfriend played in the piano bar and Kylie Minogue was stuck, like a shorter-haired Rapunzel, many floors above, grappling with the onslaught of fame and, by day, attempting to film the screen adaptation of *The Delinquents*.

Kylie, with her famous eighties perm loosened a little for the fifties setting, played the feisty Lola, who gets knocked down repeatedly but keeps dragging herself back up, and who often doesn't know where her next quid is coming from. I later read that Kylie made $13 million that year. In her own way, though, she was being buffeted by her circumstances: staying in the hotel under an assumed name, having jeans brought in when she needed a pair because it was no longer feasible for her to shop, trying to manage a private life while being pulled in all directions publicly. There must have been times when, despite her good fortune, she wondered if and when her life might start to make sense again.

Kylie was twenty at the start of production—the same age as Lola at the end of *The Delinquents*—and she turned twenty-one during the shoot. I hung around the fringes of the birthday party that the cast and crew threw for her in the hotel, before she flew to her official twenty-first in Melbourne.

At some point during my time on the periphery of the production, desperate to connect with any kind of writing community and to soak up what I could about the film business, I asked one of the producers why they'd chosen to film in Brisbane. He told me, wearily, that I wasn't the first person in town to wonder. And he told me that *The Delinquents* was a Brisbane novel.

Why did it take a multi-million-dollar film and the presence of Kylie Minogue to teach me that?

Brisbane was not then in the habit of celebrating its literature. It was a place writers left, and wrote disparagingly about from exile. If that's not entirely true, it's often how it felt. Thea Astley, David Malouf, Thomas Shapcott, Rodney Hall—the list goes on. David Malouf's *Johnno* had arrived in the mid-seventies, and was immediately taught in the classroom next to mine by a daring young English teacher who went on to lead the Democrats in the Senate. But where was *The Delinquents*?

Criena Rohan had died in 1963, a year after the book's publication. She was not, in my years growing up in Brisbane, known as one of the city's writers in exile. She wasn't even from there. But her eye for the place, and her feel for its breezes and smells and seaminess, are true. *The Delinquents* is a landmark piece of Brisbane fiction that should stand beside *Johnno* as an account of life in the city in the mid-twentieth century.

A landmark, but not an edifice. One of the book's strengths is its connection with the details of the troubled lives within it, and its pursuit of the stories of characters whom the civic leaders of the time would have wished to keep invisible. Lola and Brownie are two outsiders who find each other in their teens and who remain determined to be together, despite their families, society and the law continuing to find ways to pull them apart. In some respects *The Delinquents* feels less like a shelfmate to *Johnno* and more like Brisbane's *Last Exit to Brooklyn*, with its Spring Hill scenes of sailors and sex workers and run-ins with the cops. Hubert Selby Jr's novel was published two years after *The Delinquents*, and like Rohan's pulls no punches in depicting the rough lives of those on the margins of urban life.

The Delinquents refutes the nostalgia for a benign place where men wore hats to drive and everybody thanked the bus driver. It exposes the gap between the law and domestic conduct, and shows neighbours' backs turning on violence within families. It reveals the horrors of pregnancy termination conducted outside the law yet alongside the proper lives in Queen Street, as the black Humber arrives to take the young woman to the pitiless room where the procedure is performed.

Lola and Brownie show us the everyday dishonesty, double standards and cruelty that lurked behind the brighter images of Brisbane in the fifties. It wasn't all milk bars, big skirts and dances at Cloudland. Hugh Lunn's 1989 memoir of the era, *Over the Top with Jim*, drew readers in their hundreds of thousands; *The Delinquents* shows a different Brisbane only streets away from the Lunns' Annerley Junction bakery.

It also hints at the Queensland to come—the Queensland of the seventies and eighties, with the civil strife and the rottenness that Fitzgerald and others would drag into the light. '"If you ask me, all Brisbane's full of coppers and all of them bastards," [Lola] said, expressing in one concise sentence the full theory of central government of the sunshine state.'

The police are brutal enforcers in *The Delinquents*, and Lola and Brownie have grown up with targets on their backs. When they are caught in a pub, Brownie's fined for underage drinking and bound not to contact Lola for twelve months, while she's treated as a vagrant—a criminal offence—and put in Jacaranda Flats Girls' Corrective School.

Later, stuck in the stifling care of Auntie Westbury, at tea with one of her successfully reformed young women, Lola bristles against the tedium of suburban convention:

> Lola drank her tea and looked through the kitchen window. The success and Auntie went on to discuss the success's kitchen garden, which, it appeared, was doing 'real well', but was much plagued by the snails, so the success was going to get a couple of those, what do they call them? Muscovy ducks to eat them up. And the success was knitting harelip a lovely fair-isle jumper, and Auntie became quite animated at the mention of fair-isle. On and on it went. All the old and beautiful arts of cooking and sewing and making a home swamped in a sea of banality that was too cloying to be quite real, even taking into account the two protagonists. It was unbelievable. It sounded like a programme to teach New Australian women English.

Twenty years on, the Saints would be roaming the same inner-suburban streets as Lola and Brownie had, crafting hard, fast music that found its place at the vanguard of punk, daubing '(I'm) Stranded' on the dirty wall over the broken fireplace of an abandoned terrace house and performing community-hall shows until police arrived to shut them down. The Saints' music would have come as a shock—and not a pleasant one—to Lola and Brownie, but propelling it is a disaffectedness and disenchantment that they would have recognised all too well.

How Brooklyn has changed since Hubert Selby Jr's novel. How Brisbane has changed since *The Delinquents*—but there's still a thread linking the troubled misfit characters of these books to the present. Though some details of their lives are different, these characters are still here. Even when the system tries to be more benign, there are people in our suburbs still falling foul of it, still having to look over their shoulders.

Reviewers in the UK and Australia praised *The Delinquents* upon its publication in 1962. Yet its author was already dying. Criena Rohan was on an oxygen machine when she finished her second novel, *Down by the Dockside*, and didn't live to see the book published. She pushed on and wrote the now-lost manuscript *The House with the Golden Door*, determined to keep developing as a writer though her time was limited. Her early death cut short a significant literary career.

The Delinquents dropped from sight for most of us, but it keeps resurfacing. A new edition was published in 1986, just as film development was underway, and the following year David Bowie observed that the novel would make a good movie. That film might have pushed Lola and Brownie back into public consciousness in a lasting way, but it wasn't to be.

It was no failure domestically, grossing $3 million—a figure most current Australian productions can only dream of—but other films came along and we talked about them more, and for longer. Ben Mendelsohn, who would have made a brilliant Brownie, was apparently let go in the hope that an American lead would open up the American market. The role went to Charlie Schlatter, but the film was never released in the US. It's Lola and Brownie's story writ large—high hopes, big dreams, battlers against the tide.

Lola and Brownie and their world are too real and too compelling for us to relinquish. Every place and time needs stories of its outsiders, its rule breakers, people the establishment contrives to civilise or crush. It's the business of novelists to give these people a voice and, in *The Delinquents*, Criena Rohan's writing does that now as well as it ever did.

The Delinquents

One morning when Brownie was sixteen he put a pound (his only pound) in his money belt, kissed his mother goodbye and went off to sea. On the tram into the city he had to crack the pound to pay his fare. He went aboard the *Dalton* at eight o'clock and she sailed straight away. He was disappointed to learn that they were bound for Sydney; he had hoped for Rio de Janeiro, or at least San Francisco, and he was sea-sick as soon as they got outside Moreton Bay. Nevertheless he was happy—he was learning to be a sailor, he had got away from his mother, he was off on his search to find Lola. The sea-sickness would soon pass; the bosun assured him so.

'Work it off, that's the best thing,' he said.

So Brownie spent the day cleaning out the scuppers and thinking about Lola.

'Perhaps she'll be in Sydney anyway,' he told himself.

He had looked for her all over Brisbane, but he had not seen her since the day, twelve months before, when he had stood between two detectives on the Maryborough Station and watched her through the train window. She had stopped crying but there were tears on her cheeks, and she looked straight ahead ignoring the policewoman who sat beside her.

When the detectives had taken him back to Bundaberg his mother wept all over him and said she forgave him. The senior detective had talked to him and said he was a lucky boy to have such a good home and understanding mother. The next morning he had gone around to the hotel where Lola and her mother lived, but he was told they had left town. Only Paddy Murphy, the useful, had taken pity on him.

'Lola will be all right,' he said. 'Her mother's taking her to Brisbane to get rid of the kid.'

Brownie walked away and a little later found he was leaning against a wall weeping tears of anger and fear—anger because Lola had not wanted to get rid of the baby, fear because he knew nothing of abortion; it was just something deadly dangerous, something to be spoken of with hushed breath. Dozens of women died that way and that was all he knew.

'We'll be happy,' Lola had said. 'We'll get a wedding-ring and anyone would take you for old enough to be married, you're nearly six feet tall.'

That seemed a long time ago. Since the detectives and the policewoman had caught up with them on the Maryborough Station he had not been happy at all. Sometimes it had surprised him that a human being could exist in such bleak and uncompromising misery, and then, suddenly, ancestral memory showed him his means of escape, the refuge of generations of Hansen men—he would go to sea. From then on he became impervious to his mother. He would sit listening to her endless counsel and warnings without a word of argument, his mind busy with some cloudlike future in which he would find Lola and they would be together always. He would be captain of his own ship. That part of the dream never varied. Lola's role demanded more versatility. Sometimes she was a weeping bride being forced into a wealthy marriage by her mother. He would bear her away from the altar steps. Sometimes she was a rich widow who had never found love in her marriage: 'I never forgot you, Brownie...' Sometimes (and this was his favourite dream) she was in direst distress and poverty. He would arrive just in time to prevent some awful tragedy. But when he came back to real-life thinking he knew that he could not wait till he was Captain Hansen. He must find her quickly.

'Perhaps she'll be here in Sydney,' he thought as they sailed past North Head. 'She always said she wanted to see Sydney.' But he did not find her.

There is no sadder business than wandering around a strange town looking for a lost love, telling yourself, 'Perhaps she will be at this corner; perhaps when I turn into that street I'll find her. Perhaps she will be eating in this café. Perhaps she went past in that taxi.'

Going into shops and telling your pitiful lies.

'I'm looking for a girl who used to live in this street.' (For some streets exercised a terrible compulsion on him:

5

'She lives here,' they would cry. 'Ask for her here or you will never find her again.') 'I forget what number she lived at, but her name is Lola Lovell. She has long black hair and a scar on her right wrist.'

Then the shopkeeper shakes her head.

'No one like that round here, I'm afraid. Of course, I don't take notice of everyone who comes in. Just know the regulars.'

Sometimes they became suspicious of a boy in a leather jacket and blue jeans, and asked:

'Why don't you go to the police?'

The first time Brownie was asked that question he went out into the streets and laughed.

He became moody and had his backside kicked for it several times, for moodiness is not encouraged in deck boys. He bought the leather jacket in Sydney and the jack-knife in Melbourne, and always wore them when he went ashore. Big Emil the Norske said he had the makings of a good seaman. He kept so quiet when they spoke of women that his shipmates decided that he must be a virgin, loath to reveal his ignorance. Virginity is fraught with dangers aboard ship, so the first night back in Brisbane they decided to buy him a woman. He remembered drinking in a round of hotels, and in some lounge or other they collected the woman—a real old sailor's sweetheart dating from the time of Lord Nelson. They put her into a taxi with Brownie and packed them off.

'Don't let him get away,' they said.

He was too drunk to care very much, and once alone with the woman it was a case of *noblesse oblige*—after all his mates had paid her. When he awoke sober and saw her in the daylight he rose and dressed and went back to the ship without waking her. She slept on in the tumbled bed, her face blotchy and obscene against the pillows.

Coming along the dock in the cleanness of the dawn, Brownie prayed: 'Oh God, if You are there and if You are listening, please let me find her soon, and let her be happy. Wherever she is, let her be happy.'

The following night he went home to see his mother. She greeted him tearfully, for she had read the Shipping News the previous night and knew that the *Dalton* had been in port for more than twenty-four hours. Where had Brownie been the night before?

'I was gearman,' said Brownie, falling back on a great old sailor's standby.

He further covered himself by saying that there was no phone connected to the ship, and he thought he would have to work the next night. 'I never seem to see much of my children,' said Mrs. Hansen. 'I've done nothing except stay at home and bawl my eyes out since you went away, Brownie.'

'I missed you too,' said Brownie, who was the soul of politeness. Actually he wished he had missed her. It would have seemed more normal. He wished he even cared enough about her to want to hurt her. To want to point out that as soon as she found a man to bear her company she would weep no more for her children. It was with something like pain that he realized that he felt nothing with regard to his mother, except a desire to withdraw from her as much as possible.

'Of course your sisters should not have gone off to Cairns like that,' said Mrs. Hansen. 'I'm deeply hurt. They know my health is not the best.'

Brownie's sisters, Nita and Kristine, were always leaving home. They were, respectively, seven and six years older than Brownie, and they were good, sensible and kind-hearted girls, well able to take care of themselves. What they thought of their mother Brownie did not know. They never discussed it with him. They would suddenly announce that they could not live their own lives home with their mother—then they would go. The first time it happened was in Bundaberg. Nita and Kristine had come down to Brisbane. That was in the time of Bert Price. Bert Price was the lodger (Mrs. Hansen always had lodgers, never lovers). He was short, squat and semi-illiterate, and wore horn-rimmed glasses and an apparently irremovable felt hat. He was a cockroach exterminator, which is not a romantic trade in the North—and he hated Brownie. The girls were working and old enough to leave. Brownie found the situation unbearable, but he was not quite thirteen, so he stayed at home and took to reading cowboy novels and the *Arabian Nights*. Mrs. Hansen blamed this sudden interest in literature for his increasing stupidity at school. He had been a very clever little child. Now study seemed beyond him.

'It's all this damned reading,' his mother would say again and again. 'My God, if I'd had your chances to be educated I shouldn't have wasted them. Look at your cousin Ted in the permanent public service. Do you think he wasted his time reading? No, he improved himself. Now he'll never

8

be out of a job as long as he lives. Why don't you do some grammar? Haven't you got arithmetic to learn? What about geography?' She would look scornfully at the Fitzgerald translation. 'What good will that rubbish do you?'

The only alternative to reading seemed to be to get out of the house as much as possible. His mother said he was running wild and would end up like his father, and Bert took it upon himself to perform such fatherly duties as thrashings, etc. Brownie was a big boy. At thirteen he was five feet, and taller than Bert, and he fought him with all the strength of his unset limbs; but thirteen against a heavily muscled forty is not a fair match.

Now every woman who permits her lover to beat her husband's children sacrifices them to sexual expediency. The children know this, and they never forgive her. The woman knows this also—therefore, because we must all try to live with ourselves when all is said and done, she tries to rationalize. So it was with Mrs. Hansen.

'He done it for your own good, Brownie,' she said. 'You need a father's discipline.'

Brownie turned away. He did not trust himself to speak. He could have cried with hatred and loneliness. Then one night he met Lola. Bert was away somewhere in the country, ridding some cane-farmer's house of vermin. Mrs. Hansen was in bed. Brownie climbed out of his bedroom window and went off into the frangipani-scented night. He intended walking down to the river to look at the ships, and when he was passing Harris's she spoke to him.

'Hullo, Brownie.' She was standing under Harris's oleander tree, pinning one of its flowers into her hair.

'Hullo,' he said.

He had seen her before. She went to the Convent on Bourbon Street, and the other children called her the Creamy. She had come from Singapore with her mother early in '42. That was a long time ago now, but there was still an odd sing-song lilt in her voice.

'You're Lola aren't you?' he asked, pretending that he knew nothing about her—that he had scarcely noticed her before.

'Of course I'm Lola.'

'Does your mother know you're out?'

'Does yours?'

'No,' he admitted.

'Neither does mine,' she climbed over the fence and stood on the pavement, facing him, 'but gee, Brownie, I get so bored.'

'So do I.'

Her eyes widened with surprise.

'Why do you get bored? You've got all your own house. We've only got a tiny little room at the hotel.'

'I know,' Brownie tried to explain, 'but Mum makes me go to bed early because she believes in getting up early, and if I read in bed she says it's bad for the eyes and a waste of kerosene.'

'So you nicked out, eh? O.K., so I nicked out too.' Brownie laughed.

'You're a funny girl,' he said. 'Where is your mother?'

Lola made a vague gesture.

'Gone to a party with some Yankees off the ship down at Port Alma. I don't know where the party is.'

Brownie nodded. He knew about Yankees. Before Bert Price there had been an airman, and before the airman, the Yank. That was in the days of the war. Brownie began to feel the first glimmerings of the fellow feeling that makes us wondrous kind.

'I'd better look after you,' he said. 'Where were you going?'

'Down to the river to look at the ships,' she said. 'But now I'm out I'm a little frightened. You take me, then I won't be scared. Don't you get scared out by yourself at night, Brownie?'

'Of course not,' said Brownie.

Afterwards he kept remembering things she had said as they sat on the river bank.

'Where I come from the stars are bigger than they are here, and so close, Brownie, you feel as though you could touch them with your hand.' She put up a hand in illustration and he had thought, 'Her bones are so small and gentle. Her wrists look as though I could break them with one hand,' and he wanted to put his hands under the heavy mass of her hair and lift it away from the thinness of her neck.

'My name,' she said, 'is really Lotus. My father calls me Lotus because it is the flower of faithfulness in the East. But mother always calls me Lola. She says it is enough to have Eastern blood without an Eastern name. Oh Lord, I shouldn't have told that. Promise you won't tell anyone. Mother says that here in Australia no one would ever guess.' Brownie promised. She leaned towards him so he could smell the sweetness of the oleander flower behind her ear. 'Now,' she said, 'we have a secret.'

11

'She is like a princess,' he thought, 'an Eastern Princess out of the *Arabian Nights*.'

'My father just got up one morning and went away,' she had said.

Brownie had admired her courage. He was inclined to pretend that *his* father was working on the railways in some spot so remote from what is termed civilization in Northern Queensland that it was impossible for him to get quarters for his wife and children. This was only partly true. Father was a fettler. But he was long gone and, for all his children knew, did not care if he never saw them again. They bore him no hard feelings in regard to this for they felt that their mother had asked for it. She had left home first. She had taken her children with her and gone to live with another man.

'I had to make the break,' she would say, 'and I thought I should do it before the children were old enough to understand.'

Of course, as parents will, she put this age at about five years older than she should have, and in this first *de facto* experiment of hers what hell her two prim little daughters went through, one twelve, the other eleven, no one will ever know. Brownie was only four, and even he thought it strange. They had gone away from their house; father was no longer around; the terrifying rows ceased, and they were all living outside Tully somewhere, with a share-farmer called Bob Prentice. It was a small house. A kitchen with a wood stove, two bedrooms and a verandah. Brownie slept on the verandah, and in the night the crying of the curlews terrified him. He started school at Tully. He walked two miles to school and back each day with his sisters; and then one morning he was lifted out of bed in the cold and dark, and his mother dressed him and gave him breakfast.

'We're going back to Daddy,' said Nita, as they walked through the bush carrying their suit-cases. Even Brownie had a little bundle to carry. They had to wait a long time by the roadside before the service bus arrived, and when they finally boarded it he felt somehow that people were laughing at them. He thought it was their battered suit-cases that made him feel so outcast.

'When I'm grown up,' he told himself, 'I'll have a leather suit-case with gold letters on, like Grandfather Hansen.'

So for a while longer they followed father round from one ghastly little town to the other, depending on where the railways sent him, and then suddenly he disappeared altogether, and everyone was glad. He had not come home from work sober for a long time. Mrs. Hansen, who had done incredible things to her inside in the course of several bathroom abortions, went in and out of hospital, and her husband made her an insufficient allowance which set the pattern of rigid economy in the household which Brownie came to loathe. He was not a greedy little boy. He would gladly have gone without later in the week if they could have lived with a little style on Sunday and Monday. He dearly loved things in style. Rigid, sensible carefulness galled him. All his life he hated sweet potatoes, corned beef, home hair-cuts, golden syrup, powdered milk and flour bags (they reminded him of sheets).

Then came the war, and the first lodger was called Jack. He departed for overseas, a gallant hero in a slouch hat.

13

He was not very popular, in his absence having entirely omitted to make his landlady an allowance.

'The mongrel,' she would say, 'the lousy rotten mongrel. After all I done for him.'

She cheered up with the advent of the Yank. He was a cheerful good-tempered, middle-aged man, who brought the Hansen children piles of what he called candy. Mrs. Hansen took to going dancing.

'God knows,' she would say, 'I never had any life before, stuck out there in the bush without even a wireless, coping with a drunken husband, three kids and a fallen womb.'

This, of course, was absolutely true.

The American was moved to Melbourne and then came the big adventure of Mrs. Hansen's life. Small wonder the ladies will never forget the Yanks. 'I'm sick of this joint and the evil-minded people in it,' she told her daughters one morning. 'I think I'll go South and see if we might make our home down there.'

'Why don't you?' said Nita, who was the second girl and very fond of her father. 'Please don't worry about Brownie. We'll look after him.' 'You know, Nita,' said her mother with seeming irrelevance, 'you are the image of your Grandmother Hansen. Old bitch that she was.'

So the Yank treated Mrs. Hansen to a holiday down South, and a wonderful time she had. He took her to the State Theatre which was much admired by the Yanks, and they even went to a night club. They were booked into a fairly good hotel which seemed like the Taj Mahal to Mrs. Hansen, and all the time they played a game the burden of which was that only Mrs. Hansen's impregnable respectability made divorce impossible. His tone seemed to infer that, if it were not for this, both his wife and Goran Hansen would find divorce papers served on them within the week.

Mrs. Hansen played the little game, but in many ways she was a realist. She knew that the holiday was for favours received, that the Yank would go happily back to his wife and expected her to go, if not happily, then at least resignedly, back to that God-awful little town in the sticks.

Whither Mrs. Hansen in due course went, to resign herself to middle age and to accuse her neighbours for many years to come—the virtuous along with the guilty—of 'carrying on with the Yanks during the war.'

'Most great lovers if they lived today would be considered juvenile delinquents—Helen of Troy was just twelve years old when she ran away with Paris.'

Havelock Ellis makes this wise observation. Nobody has ever tried to excuse Helen and Paris. They were great lovers. This is the end of the matter. Of Lola and Brownie, Lola was the only one who had characteristics tending to delinquency. She had an inherited love of change and excitement, which so far she had managed to sublimate by sitting alone in hotel rooms reading historical novels and all the poetry she could procure. Her mother could go to a party leaving her tucked up in bed and know that she would be there, asleep, with her head pillowed on an open book, at one, two or three in the morning, whenever the party ended. It was very convenient.

'You wouldn't know she was in the place,' her mother could say; and she felt, and all her friends felt, that surely no mother could ask for more. But adolescence came and stirred her body and tugged at her mind, and she knew she was lonely. And now the stage was set for trouble, for Lola had nourished her mind and her heart on dreams and had an innocent ruthlessness about converting her dreams into reality (and, oh, dear social worker, of all things beware the adolescent dreamer with a bit of guts). She wanted to be loved. Now she began casting Brownie in the rôle of lover, but she was physically immature, and had no real notion or fear of the tumult in the body of the boy.

She was sitting on a cross branch of their favourite frangipani tree down by the river when Brownie asked her:

'Will you go steady with me?'

And she said:

'I don't know. I'll have to think about it. You may have my hand to kiss,' and she put out her hand, feeling like Napoleon's Josephine.

Had she merely said 'O.K.,' Australian style, it would have been months before Brownie would have plucked up the courage to kiss her; but now he took the fragile Eurasian hand in his and, instead of kissing it with the courtly flourish her books had taught her to expect, he turned it over and suddenly kissed it hard on the palm. She snatched it away and they faced one another, their eyes dilating. Brownie felt that he would choke, that he would never breathe smoothly again. Then he put his hands up and at last lifted her hair away from her neck.

'Your neck,' he said, almost with wonder. 'It's warm, darling. It's so soft and warm.'

He began to kiss her then wildly all over the face and neck and the childish pointed breasts. She began to tremble, but made not one move to repulse him.

'Don't be frightened, darling,' he was saying. 'Don't be frightened. Look I won't hurt you. I'll take you home now. Don't shake, darling, don't tremble. Oh, darling, don't be frightened of me. I wouldn't hurt you. You're so special. You're such a special little thing.'

He lifted her out of the tree and it was the lightness of the small quivering body in his arms that undid them both and brought their childhood to an end there in the night amongst the long grass and the fallen flowers of the frangipani.

That was when Brownie was a month off fifteen—a big boy, almost six feet tall, who had worked like a man in every school holiday since he was twelve. What are we to do with the great overgrown lads whose bodies are a torment to them? Do the social workers and clergymen, well meaning though they be, really think youth clubs, organized sport, fretwork classes are of any use? Come now! Lola had no faith in the Boy Scouts, the young Liberal Movement, choir practice, the Junior Chamber of Commerce, cold showers (always supposing you could get a cold shower in Bundaberg), or these healthy outside interests they're always talking about. All she knew was that Brownie wanted her and loved her. He was, she decided, the only person who had ever wanted her exactly

17

as she was, without qualification and condition, therefore he should have her.

By many standards Lola was a fortunate child. True she had no settled home and her parents were separated, but against that it must be considered that she was given plenty of liberty, was never beaten nor bullied (except by the gentlest methods) and was given everything in the way of clothes and education that her mother could afford. There would have been a host of people in Bundaberg to declare that her mother was devoted to her. A hard and humiliating childhood and adolescence had left Mrs. Lovell with the conviction that to be accepted by the professional classes was the end and aim of every right-thinking woman's existence. She distrusted love and disliked men—they reminded her of Tony Lovell and she looked back on her wild infatuation for him with deepest shame. Lola, she decided, would be well educated, would have a career, would marry, if she married at all, a doctor, a lawyer, a bank manager—a man who wore a public school tie. She would have been astounded to know that one woman could create from her own flesh another so unlike herself. Lola never argued with her mother. The nuns had taught her pretty manners and, at any rate, she knew that arguing would be useless; but while her mother talked to her of the day when she would be a nurse or private secretary or doctor's receptionist, Lola dreamed of the day when she would be a ballroom-dancing instructress, or travel the country in a carnival caravan; above all, of the man who would worship her, love her, adore her. And now fate had sent along Brownie, the biggest, the handsomest, the gentlest and softest spoken boy in all the town.

Coming home on that first night she sat in the bath a long while and tried to think out the situation. She knew that if her mother knew she would be ill with shock. She knew she might already be pregnant, and, worst of all, according to all she had been taught, the fires of hell were already roaring for her, though of this last she could not be afraid. She found it so hard to believe. She gave up all attempt at coherent thought. It is impossible to reason out anything with a voice inside you, half demented with joy, shouting, 'I am loved, I am loved.'

'If mother knew,' she thought, 'she would hate me. There are dozens of things about me that mother would hate if only she knew. But whatever I do Brownie loves me. Brownie loves me.'

She was sound asleep with her cheek on her hand when her mother came home.

Brownie had never dreamed of love as an escape at all. From his own observation he had decided that all physical love was dirty—a sort of disgraceful trap into which everybody fell despite their best endeavour. He had watched his mother's lodgers come and go. Though the American had been unfailingly kind to him he had had the most traumatic effect upon the child, for on a Saturday afternoon the American would come home from camp early, and then he and Mrs. Hansen would lie on Brownie's bed (presumably because Brownie's room did not overlook the gossip-hungry street) and there make what, for want of a more appropriate word, must be called love. The Hansen children did not stay around to witness their embraces. The girls went out to tennis and made good Mrs. Hansen's boast that her girls were wonderful sensible girls, never a day's worry, mad on sports and their jobs, etc., not interested in boys and all that rubbish at all. The girls never discussed the situation, even with one another. Their humiliation was too great. They merely saved their money and left home as soon as they could. Brownie, by a triumph of *dementia praecox*, often managed to convince himself that it was not happening at all. He would ride away on his bike on a Saturday afternoon and behind him there was nothing— just a vacuum devoid of love, truth or happiness.

'I'd be frightened I wouldn't like a Sheila any more after I'd done that,' he had once said to a more experienced friend who was boasting. But it had not been like that at all. He was already so far gone in revolt against his mother, and Lola was such a polar type to that loud-voiced, fair-skinned, big-framed woman that Lola could do no wrong. Her every word, action and look was a source of beauty and joy to him. He found he was walking around half dazed with the remembrance of the gentleness of her love-making, the fragility of her bones and the darkness of her eyes in the shadows beneath the trees. There was no room in his heart for any feeling of disgust or disgrace.

'She is beautiful,' the voice within him cried. 'She is beautiful and she is good.'

It happened about the time when Bert Prince was at his most obnoxious that Brownie took Lola riding on his bike one evening. He would put her up on the crosspiece and thus they would go for miles, while her mother thought she was with one of her school friends, being helped with her mathematics homework. Well, on this occasion the night was so warm and still that they stayed out much longer than they had planned. Brownie took the precaution of stopping round the corner from home and letting down the back tyre, but even this was not a good enough excuse for his mother, who had been picturing his body caught in a snag in the river for the last hour or more. She fell upon him as soon as he got in the door and administered two heavy slaps across the head, and Brownie, who always felt his body purified by Lola's love-making said:

'Get your frigging hand off me.'

Mrs. Hansen gasped and stepped back. Bert rose from his chair.

'You'll respect your mother, boy,' he said.

'That's right,' cried Brownie, in a terrible parody of Bert's portentousness. 'Never mind love, I can do what I like, but I'll see everyone else respects you.' He laughed. 'Good old Bert, seeing that everyone does the right thing by the poor weak woman. It's just like the pictures.'

Bert's fist caught him straight in the mouth.

'That's right, Bert, belt him,' said the woman.

When it was over Bert said:

'Now get up to the wood heap and cut the morning wood.'

And while Brownie was chopping the wood and crying with rage his mother came to him and said:

'It's for your own good, Brownie. You're growing up real bad like your father. A boy needs a man to keep him in order.'

'Get away from me,' said Brownie.

21

'You wouldn't love me, Brownie,' she said, 'if I let you get away with that. You wouldn't have no respect for me.'

'Will you get away from me?' said Brownie.

'I'm not going to let you grow up all anyhow, Brownie,' she persisted. 'If you won't do the right thing you've got to be made to.'

'Just get away from me,' said Brownie.

Mrs. Hansen went back to Bert. Her passion for self-justification and violence was aroused and she was really away.

'You'll have to go up to him again, Bert,' she said. 'He's behaving like a mad thing.'

'We'll see about that,' said Bert, and he tightened his belt and took out his false teeth and wended his way to the wood heap.

'Look here, young Hansen,' he said. 'You're going just the way of your old man, the bloody mongrel, and I'm not going to let you—your mother had to take enough off of him.'

Bert did not see fit to mention that he himself had once taken a beating from him that was still the talk of Cloncurry.

'Get away,' said Brownie.

'I'm going to get an apology from you first.'

Brownie goaded to madness threw the axe at him.

Then the fight raged, watched by Mrs. Hansen from her kitchen window and several neighbours collected in the street.

While he fought Bert realized that his days of flogging Goran Hansen's son were almost over. This time Brownie

22

was almost too much for him. So he fought as never before and each blow and kick he drove home he savoured to the full.

'Mark the good-looking bastard for life.'

All Bert's hatred of the young and beautiful and easy to love went into the blow that broke Brownie's nose, and at last, when Brownie lay half-conscious on the ground, he knelt over him, crazed with joy, and asked: 'Will you apologize now?'

Brownie shook his head and Bert raised his fist again. Mrs. Hansen, conscious of murmuring among the watching neighbours, hurried out and caught his hand.

'He's had enough, Bert,' she said.

Brownie sat up and his mother went forward to help him, but he pushed her aside and with the help of a tree trunk dragged himself to his feet. His mother took his arm.

'Forget about it now, Brownie,' she said. 'Shake hands and make up.'

Brownie shrugged his arm free. She turned to the neighbours and said, 'I don't know why you can't all get home and mind your own business.'

She held her head high and spoke intrepidly, but she knew that she had failed the only test she really feared—the awful, the merciless trial by neighbours' opinion. Brownie staggered into the house. She followed him and said: 'You'd better let me get you cleaned up, Brownie.' Her son said nothing. He went into his room and locked the door and all night he lay with the blood caking on his body and every limb and muscle hardening into pain. Several times they knocked on his door and he answered:

'Get away, just get away from me for ever.'

Lola heard the story the next day. The Ryans lived next door to the Hansens and the little Ryan girls came to school full of it. Bert Prince had battered Brownie unconscious and Mrs. Hansen had stood by and encouraged him. It lost nothing in the telling. Lola waited for Brownie at their usual place on the river bank that evening, but he did not come. She waited till it was quite dark and then she made up her mind what she must do and hurried back to the hotel.

'Mother,' she asked, 'may I go to the pictures with Hazel Ryan?'

Her mother said yes, she always did, and Lola set off back again towards Alton Street and the Ryans' house. But she did not go into the Ryans'.

She wrigged quickly between the broken pickets that formed the Hansen's back fence and climbed into the Moreton Bay fig tree that grew higher than the house. She climbed as high as she could and then settled down, hidden by the branches, to watch till all the lights went out. 'I'll give them about half an hour after that,' she thought, 'and then I'll get in through Brownie's window.'

She had not so long to wait. She was hardly settled before Mrs. Hansen and Bert came out and set off towards town. Lola slid out of the trees and ran. No creeping in through Brownie's window. She swept straight in through the kitchen door demanding:

'Brownie, why did you stand me up?'

'What are you doing here?'

'Looking for you—you great big, ugly old stand-up merchant.' She sat down on the bed and put her arms around him.

'I heard all about it, Brownie,' she said, 'and Hazel Ryan said you gave him plenty to go on with. So now why did you leave me waiting on that damned old river bank?'

Brownie looked at the floor between his feet.

'I didn't want you to see my face,' he said.

'Ah, so that's it. I thought that would be the trouble. That's why I'm so angry with you. Gee, I'll give you a flogging when I get my strength up.'

But Brownie did not laugh. He just sat staring at the floor.

'Oh, come off it, Brownie. If you're in trouble you've got to come to me. We made a bargain.'

'Look,' said Brownie, 'I've had to ride around town all day delivering blasted telegrams with everyone peering on my face. I've felt like the Phantom of the bloody Opera, I couldn't bear you to see it. Look, Lola, Mum won't even let me go to the doctor. She says it's nothing and I should put hot compresses on it, but she's only frightened of the Welfare. She doesn't want a doctor to see it in case he says something. But I met Paddy Murphy, you know the "useful" at your pub, and he had a look at it and he says it's broken all right. Not the bone but the Septum.'

'What's that?' Lola looked, dubiously, at the poor swollen nose.

'It's the flesh at the end of the nose.'

'Well that's not as bad as the bone,' comforted Lola.

'It's bad enough. Anyway I wouldn't expect any girl to stick to me if I had a nose like Paddy Murphy.'

Lola began to laugh.

'Let's not lose our sense of humour,' she said. 'Paddy's nose has been broken dozens of times by some of the hardest punchers in the world. Bert isn't that good.'

'He gave me a hell of a hiding,' said Brownie.

Lola stood up and cradled the boy's battered head against her breast. Her eyes, always slightly tilted, were now narrow slits and elongated with rage but she spoke softly, almost dreamily, and she ran her hands very gently through the brown curls.

'Your hair is still beautiful as ever,' she said, and then, as though the prowess of Bert Prince was only worthy of discussion as an afterthought:

'He's got a shiner himself, and in a couple of years, Brownie, we'll meet up with him, and by that time you'll be full grown, and then nothing will save him; between us we'll kill him.' She turned his head up towards her and kissed him hard on the mouth.

'I don't care if I hurt you,' she said, taking his face between her hands. 'Oh, Brownie, I love you. I wouldn't care if he'd turned your face right round. I want you because you gave the big bastard a good run for his money, and in a couple of years you'll be able to eat him.' And then she was lying on the bed and Brownie was weeping with his head against her breast and then her mouth found his.

Quickly it flowed into her body driving away his hurt. A soft warm wave—the healing and rebirth of love and possession.

And in that moment Lola conceived his son.

She went back to the hotel, told her mother the pictures had been wonderful, went to bed and slept dreamlessly, worn out and happy with the satisfying work of re-creating a man—and then in the morning as she awoke panic hit her in an icy wave, for she and Brownie had been careless. Previously Brownie had always been as careful of her as he knew how. He had gained what knowledge of contraception he had from a school friend, Harry Gwynn, another big, overgrown boy, a little older than Brownie, who had been having a very satisfactory affair for some years with a nymphomaniacal school-teacher who had seduced him when he was thirteen. Brownie had left school the day he was fifteen and was now a telegraph boy, with a certain amount of money to spend as he liked each week; so, under Harry's direction, he had spent some of it in buying a supply of one of the more old-fashioned soluble pessaries. When supplies and money ran out simultaneously, Harry stole some for him while at night school, as he put it. It is possible that Lola would not have escaped pregnancy very long with only such primitive protection, but they are better than nothing, and on that night neither she nor Brownie had remembered them.

At the end of two weeks of agonised waiting she knew that she was pregnant. Then, suddenly, she did not care any more.

'I'll give it another month to make sure,' she told herself, for she was still young enough and hopeful enough to believe all those old chestnuts about colds, shocks, upsets, etc. 'And then I'll tell him.'

Lola and Brownie sat looking at the river.

'Do you want to get rid of it?' asked Brownie.

27

'Good grief, no,' Lola cried out in alarm, 'that would be a terrible mortal sin.'

Brownie said no more. He was very careful of people's religious susceptibilities, particularly Catholics who seemed to get up in arms over the strangest things—besides, he had not really wanted to get rid of it himself. One thing must be said for our adolescents; they have a good old-fashioned human horror of abortion. In a land where the woman with a large family is considered somewhat of a fool (if not downright indecent), and yet to terminate a pregnancy is so utterly illegal, it is only to be expected that from earliest childhood they have heard whispers of home surgery with details so horrible that they would raise a shudder in the Emperor Nero himself.

So now Brownie said, suddenly feeling master of the situation:

'O.K., we'll have to go away.'

'Have you saved anything?' asked Lola.

'Not much, and Mum keeps my bank book, but I can get some off Jimmy Lim.'

Jimmy Lim was an old Chinese who had a market garden on the outskirts of the town. Brownie had spent a lot of time sitting with the fowls in Jimmy's indescribable kitchen—eating candied ginger and listening to stories that were as good as the Voyages of Marco Polo—and his school mates, out of deference to this eccentricity, refrained from robbing Jimmy's trees. Jimmy rose to the occasion. He dug up the ground in front of his fireplace and gave Brownie twenty-five pounds. Harry Gwynn also came forward with a little going-away present; the wedding-ring that his teacher love always used when she went down to Brisbane with the bank manager. Harry had removed it from the top drawer of her dressing-table, which he knew his way around, by long practice, as well as he knew his way round Bundaberg. Then he had kissed her good night and gone home. He presented it to Brownie with a flourish next morning.

'You shouldn't steal off her,' said Brownie.

Harry waved his objection aside. 'Go on, take it,' he said. 'She's only a bag when all is said and done.'

Harry was a bit of a moralist in his own way.

Brownie pocketed the ring with a look of unwilling admiration. 'You bludger,' he told his friend.

He and Lola set off the next day. Brownie left a note which merely said:

'Dear Mum, I've gone away. Please do not worry and do not set the police after me. I've got money and I'll be all right. I'll write soon, Brownie.'

But Lola, romantically read, must go writing in more traditional vein.

'Dear Mother,' said her note, 'I am going to have a baby. I am going anywhere I will not be a humiliation to you. I am well looked after, etc., etc.' Lola enjoyed writing that note.

'Someone loves me and wants to look after me.' She wished she could shout it in the street.

The two mothers arrived at the police station within seconds of each other, and when they met and saw that they were both clutching a note, both notes written on pages torn from the same exercise book, all was made clear as the saying goes, and both ladies fell to—Mrs. Hansen grim and righteous and Mrs. Lovell hysterical. Each blamed the other's child. Mrs. Hansen called Lola a dirty little half-bred, over-sexed slut, no better than the bloody blacks and cunning as a shit-house rat. Mrs. Lovell said that Brownie was a great big over-sexed Norwegian.

'My God, how I hate Norwegians,' she screamed. She did, too. Their guiltless attitude towards sex had always infuriated her. Mrs. Hansen said:

'Don't you speak about my boy like that!'

And Mrs. Lovell shrieked:

'You should care. You're the talk of Bundaberg. You let your customers beat up your precious boy. I wish they'd killed him,' she added illogically.

Then was Mrs. Hansen indeed infuriated because she had given Bert his marching orders more than a month ago.

'Bert,' she had said, 'you'll have to go—people are talking.'

Bert knew that in a small town there is no arguing with this most powerful of all reasons. So he went, and Mrs. Hansen had not taken long to persuade herself that she was the most devoted of mothers who had broken off the romance of a lifetime for the sake of her children—and here was this bitch yelling about customers. It is possible that Mrs. Lovell would, within a few minutes, have had the supreme pleasure of charging Mrs. Hansen with assault had the police not intervened and brought them back to the business of the missing children's description, etc.

On the train bound for Brisbane Lola kept twirling the ring on her finger.

'I feel really and truly happy and really and truly married,' she confided to Brownie. 'Do you think everything will be all right?'

Brownie smiled and dropped one arm lazily around her. 'For sure it will,' he said.

He believed it too. He was as big as a man and could work like a man, and jobs were not hard to get, and Lola had a wedding-ring, and when she had the baby she could play with it like a doll and he would work for them both. This prospect filled his Scandinavian soul with joy. And they had twenty-five pounds to go on with.

'Love and freedom,' sang the wheels of the train. 'Love and freedom, love and freedom.'

The police put an end to all that nonsense—they caught up with them at Maryborough.

There were two plain-clothes police and a policewoman in uniform. They found Brownie and Lola in the railway refreshment rooms. Brownie was fetching two cups of tea from the counter and Lola sat at a table, her arms full of chocolates, peanuts, potato crisps, popcorn and other foods highly recommended for expectant mothers.

Brownie saw them first and put the tea down and stood with his back to the counter. He knew in that most hideous moment of his life that he was about to lose Lola for a long while, perhaps for ever, and he determined to fight as long as he could. So he fought like a wild animal, but it did not take long, for one policeman bravely kicked him in the groin and as he bent over to shield his agonized body the other clipped him smartly under the jaw, and even as the darkness rose to meet him, his eyes found Lola—she had

31

ceased to struggle with the policewoman. She stood sobbing bitterly with sweets and peanuts strewn around her feet and a broken bag of popcorn shaking in her hands.

When Brownie came to he found he was still in the refreshment rooms. They had put him in a chair and he sat slumped with his head hanging between his knees, and a cane-cutter was being restrained by his more sober friends from coming to his rescue. Slowly he straightened himself and looked at the police. Lola and the policewoman had gone. He knew as surely as if he had been told that at that moment they were getting into the train going up to Bundaberg.

'Can I watch them go?'

The bigger of the two policemen nodded. He walked out on to the station. It had come on to rain. Lola and the policewoman sat in a carriage almost opposite him and the policewoman was talking to Lola.

Lola looked straight ahead. Her profile looked defiant and amazingly sad, and the rain made tears on the carriage window.

When Mrs. Lovell took Lola down to Brisbane she took her straight to a leading gynaecologist who gave his opinion that Lola would probably miscarry in any case.

'She's much too small and too young,' he said.

'I can't afford to take the chance,' said Mrs. Lovell, and she dragged the terrified child to an abortionist whose address she had procured from a policeman who drank in the hotel where they were staying. The abortionist was a qualified doctor, conscientious and kind according to his lights.

'She is too far gone,' he said. 'I don't touch anyone over eight weeks.'

Then the waitress at the hotel took pity on them one morning when Lola suddenly vomited her bacon and eggs on to the dining-room floor and her mother fell on her beating her with clenched fists and shrieking:

'You filthy little bitch, I wish you would die.'

The waitress looked at Lola with complete sympathy and understanding.

'I know a woman out at New Farm who's very good,' she said, 'and she only charges a tenner.'

Mrs. Lovell's heart quailed at the mention of this price cutting.

'I don't care how much it costs,' she said. 'I'd pay £100 for a good doctor if only I could find one.'

'I'm not here,' Lola told herself. 'I'm somewhere else. All this is not happening.' And she began to experience a feeling that she was soon to know all too well, that she was floating out of herself. That one Lola Lovell was seated on a chair watching the waitress clean up the floor but that she herself—her real self—was floating away. Floating peacefully, looking down at the poor sick girl in the chair. It was a relaxing feeling, but frightening also. From her disembodied haven she heard the waitress say,

'This woman is good. Honest she's real good and clean—washes her hands in Dettol and everything.'

Mrs. Lovell shuddered again.

That evening Mrs. Lovell, who had been drinking most of the afternoon with the young policeman, announced that she was going to dinner with him.

'You stay where you are,' she told Lola, 'and don't go rambling out into the streets picking up men. I'd rather stay in, Heaven knows I'm in no mood for dining out, but Tom says he may be able to put me on to someone else. I'm doing this for you.'

So off she went with the rookie cop who wasted a lot of liquor and made a sad mess of himself before he learned that Mrs. Lovell could drink him well under the table before she even thought of becoming amorous; and Lola, who was too shaken and nervy to go down to the dining-room by herself went out and bought a chocolate bar that made her feel slightly sick again, and a magazine which she found she could not read. She tried blankly gazing at pages which she knew her eyes had read and her mind had ignored, and in the end she threw it on the bed and went and stood by the window weeping with her head against the pane.

'Oh, Brownie,' she sobbed. 'Brownie—Oh, Brownie, oh, Brownie.'

She was standing like this when the waitress knocked at the door.

'I've found another name for you, love,' said the waitress. 'My girl friend told me. It's a doctor, too, but you ring the nurse.'

'I don't want to,' sobbed Lola. 'My mother's making me.'

'Mother knows best,' said the waitress with unconscious humour.

The voice was cheerful, educated and above all business-like. The first thing it said was: 'Have you forty-five pounds?'

'Yes.'

'Just put them in an envelope, cash you know, not a cheque, with your name on it and bring it with you.'

'Very well.'

'Now you'll need six Modess pads. Wrap them in a clean handkerchief.'

'Yes.'

'And a new sanitary belt and a large bottle of Dettol. Are you writing down what I'm saying?'

'Yes.'

'Good girl! Now I want you to get some calcium tablets and take three after each meal till Wednesday morning.'

'Yes, I'll do that.'

'Now on Wednesday morning don't have any breakfast and be waiting by the letter-box on the corner of Albert and Queen Streets at 9.45 a.m. A black Humber will pick you up at 10 a.m. The last three letters of its registration number will be 219. Have you got all that?'

'Yes.'

'The car will drop you back at the letter-box at three in the afternoon. Good, well I'll see you Wednesday morning, dear. Goodbye now.'

'Goodbye.'

Lola came out of the phone box and leaned against the wall, her legs shaking with fright. These cloak and dagger arrangements terrified her beyond measure. She saw herself, of course, being dropped by the same sinister black Humber not back at the letter-box, safe and sound and living, but into the river in the dead of Wednesday night, a corpse and nobody any the wiser.

'I *cannot* do it,' she kept telling herself. 'No, I just cannot go through with it. Something will happen to stop it, or I'll run away or something like that.'

Again she had the terrible feeling that she was on some other plane than everyone else. That if she spoke like this they would not hear her, or at least would not know what she was talking about. So she walked about like a figure in a nightmare telling herself over and over again:

'It won't happen because I couldn't live through it. It won't happen to me.'

But on Wednesday morning there she was with her mother, waiting at the letter-box, and when the nightmare Humber drew up at the kerb it was driven by a young man with so friendly a smile that she was emboldened to ask:

'May my mother come too?'

'Certainly, kiddie,' said the driver. 'Here, you hop in the front and we'll pack Mum in the back.'

There were two other girls in the car and the one in the back began to cry.

'I wish my mother was here,' she sobbed.

'Well,' said the other, 'I'm bloody glad mine's not.'

Lola was almost three months gone so they curetted her without anaesthetic. She put her hands in her mouth and tried not to cry out, and the nurse said,

'Good girl, you behaved well for a first-timer.'

The nurse, though considerably de-humanized by her job, was not a bad nor an unkind woman, and she was glad that Lola fainted with pain and grief and did not see Brownie's child being carted away to the incinerator in an enamel bucket.

'Was it a little boy?' asked Lola when she regained consciousness.

'Neither,' lied the abortionist. 'It's nothing yet—just like a lump of blood. There's no life till it moves.'

He went off to wash his hands and then attend to the next patient. The nurse gave Lola a cup of tea and sent out to her mother. Mrs. Lovell was rather drunk, having primed herself with nips from the brandy flask she carried in her bag.

'You could have saved your money,' said the nurse, 'that child is far too small to carry a child past about four months.'

'I always took good care of her,' said Mrs. Lovell.

She looked up and saw Lola standing white-faced in the doorway.

'My baby,' she said, and held out her arms.

Lola did not move: she stood looking at her mother.

'It's all over now, darling,' said Mrs. Lovell nervously.

'Yes,' said Lola, 'everything's over. I would like a cigarette.'

The nurse helped her across the room to her mother.

'Let her sit in that armchair a minute,' she said to Mrs. Lovell, 'and give her a nip of that brandy—that is,' she added, 'if there's any left.'

Mrs. Lovell adopted her best mem sahib manner and bade the nurse not to be insolent and to ring a taxi for her daughter.

Lola had a nip of brandy and began to feel that one day she would be warm again.

'Goodbye,' said the nurse. 'Get her to bed when you get home and if anything goes wrong get her to the General and remember—she fell down the stairs.'

But nothing went wrong. At least nothing that warranted a visit to the General. Lola lay in bed for a couple of days suffering from shock and weeping a great deal in a quiet helpless sort of way. These tears annoyed her mother who kept on saying:

'It's all over now.'

And rather more briskly:

'You want to pull your socks up, my lady. There's no point in feeling sorry for yourself for the rest of your life, you know.'

Mrs. Lovell herself, now the worst was over, was beginning to relish the situation. She saw herself as a mother who had violated her deepest religious principles to succour an erring daughter. As she put it to the young policeman:

'I got Lola through it, but at a tremendous sacrifice.'

The lounge of the hotel was filled from about eleven in the morning onwards with ladies who had gone through similar trials—either on their own behalf or that of a friend or daughter. A woman's lot was hard. It needed sustaining with a great deal of hard liquor. It was all very cosy and friendly there in the lounge, swapping stories of their sufferings at the hands of the common enemy—men. Women had a lot to put up with, men were bastards and kids! My God, kids were a worry. Mrs. Lovell was the heroine of the hour, the real nice woman, deserted by the worthless husband; the woman who'd given the best years of her life to educating her daughter, best of education the kid had been given, and then this had to happen. They sighed into their beer, they shook their heads over their gin—they went home to nag their children and grudgingly sling chops and three vegetables at the clods of husbands who did not realize what treasures they had won.

This was all very well for a couple of days. Then the publican's wife grew restive. She had had her eye on the husky young policeman herself, for the publican, though he could drink all day without any visible effect, had usually rendered himself impotent by bedtime, and she felt that young policeman could have been better employed than in buying Mrs. Lovell's drinks and sitting there hanging on every word she uttered in that clipped, phoney English accent. So on Friday evening the publican's wife said they must go. She pretended to have only just discovered the truth about Lola.

'I won't have people resting up here after illegal operations,' she said. 'I won't have that sort of thing in my pub. You'll have to have her out by ten tomorrow morning.'

Lola, once up on her feet, was faint and shaky—also hemorrhaging badly, if not dangerously. But go she must. The publican's wife watched her depart without pity. 'Think yourself lucky I don't get the police,' she said.

'I could get the police too,' she told her husband that night; and then, with rage that she herself could not understand, 'The little whore, I hope she bleeds to death.'

Late on the Saturday afternoon Mrs. Lovell took a job as a drink-waitress in a South Side hotel. She and Lola were to share a dark and somewhat airless room up at the back of the third floor.

'I think I'll get my daughter to bed right away,' she told the manager, 'she's had a bad attack of flu.'

Later on that same evening Mrs. Hansen paused in the act of pouring tea and said to her son:

'It's no good going on like this, refusing to eat. It's over now, and any rate I think we'll move. I don't like taking you away just when you got into the Post Office and all, but I don't fancy staying here now you've given them something to talk about.'

'I haven't told anyone,' protested Brownie.

'It'll get around. Things always do in a town this size. That filthy little bitch's mother was spilling her guts all over the place. That's one thing you should think of before you play up, Brownie—it's your people who suffer.'

'Yes indeed,' said Brownie.

So Brownie arrived in Brisbane about two months after Lola. He got a job in a rubber factory and moved, with his mother, into a flat in the Valley. Then he started to look for her. He looked for her amongst groups of schoolgirls and in the crowds in picture theatres. He went to parks and up and down the river. Sometimes he thought he saw her ahead of him in the street and then he would run to catch up with her, but when he came abreast he would see it was not Lola at all; some pitiful trick of his hopeful imagination had made him think there was something the same about the carriage of the head or the turn of the neck. Sometimes his heart would come into his mouth when he would think he saw her walking with a man—but it would not be Lola after all. Just a girl, hanging on someone's arm as Lola had hung on his.

Mrs. Hansen, consumed with anxiety as never before, now took it upon herself to lecture and warn him every night. She warned him to save, she warned him about women, she warned him against girls and about venereal disease. Night after night as she sat and sewed her voice went on and on, filling the kitchen with fear and Brownie did not listen. He had withdrawn from his mother for ever. She would never touch him again. He found he could sit and think quite comfortably while the tide of his mother's ignorance, superstition and insecurity flowed around him.

'You know, Brownie, you want to be careful of the drink. I was never a wowser but I'd be just as glad if you never touched it. Look at your father. Look at those old pensioners you see outside the wine shops on pension day. You know it's in you. That's why I'm warning you. I'm only telling you. I've told the girls too. Of course Kristine's all right, but Nita gets real upset. You have to be real careful what you say to Nita, but it's my duty. I just showed her an old woman sitting in the gutter outside one of these plonk shops in the Bight. She was helpless. She couldn't scratch herself. It was dreadful to think a woman could fall so low, and I just said to Nita "Any one of us could come to it, Nita; you want to always remember that. The weakness is in you from your father," I said...'

Brownie said 'Yes, Mum' and 'No, Mum' at regular intervals, and thought it was not to be wondered at that the girls had gone back up North, and wished he had enough money to go to the pictures, and wished his job were not so dull, and wished he had something to read, and wished he could find Lola.

Meanwhile Lola's mother had decided she would send her daughter back to school and Lola had gone, apathetic but unprotesting; but it had not been a success. She could not concentrate; she lost weight; she made no friends, and she took to waking in the night, shaking and sobbing. The doctor said she was on the verge of a nervous breakdown and must have rest. After that she moped around the hotel reading magazines, crying and sleeping.

Then she began to go around with Kath. Kath cleaned out the bedrooms and helped in the bar at rush hours. She was neither very intelligent nor particularly kind, but she had the one good point of never questioning anything that anyone did and Lola found this restful. The first time they went out together they merely went to the pictures and had supper with a couple of national servicemen whom Kath seemed to know well—indeed she seemed to know every Nasho in Brisbane.

'What did you think of those two?' she asked Lola next morning.

Lola shrugged.

'I'm not keen on Nashos,' she said. 'I prefer bodgies.'

Once, about six months after he went to sea, they almost found each other. It was in the lounge of the Grand Hotel.

Brownie went round from the front bar to pick up a couple of bottles of wine from the bottle department. He stood in the lounge doorway drunk and very handsome, looking the field over and wondering if it would be worth while picking up a woman, or if he would go back on board and drink the sherry, and then the woman picked him up. She rose unsteadily from her chair, put her arm through his and said:

'Come on, Johnny, let's go.'

Lola was inside in the toilet being very sick. She came out no more than thirty feet behind Brownie and the woman, but she saw nothing—nothing except the ground heaving beneath her feet and the stars falling out of the sky. She clung to the hotel wall vomiting and weeping and exclaiming:

'Christ, I'm drunk. Oh hell, I'm drunk. I'm bloody, stinking drunk.'

She looked as unpleasant a little delinquent as ever made a policeman's mouth water. From this predicament she was rescued by a shearer who was staying at her hotel. He got her into a taxi and took her home to her mother.

'You'll want to take better care of her,' he told Mrs. Lovell, who was having a good-night beer in the kitchen with the Chef and the Manager.

Mrs. Lovell went into the usual old mother-love routine, with the manager echoing her like a Greek chorus.

'At any rate,' she concluded, 'I do not propose to have a common shearer dictate to me.'

The common shearer laughed in her face.

'Don't make yourself sound silly,' he advised. 'That kind of talk went out with buttoned boots. And what's so great about you. You're just a phoney kidding phonies. You haven't got education or class or self-respect or even common sense. I come from where there are still a few real ladies kicking around, and they're recognized as such even

43

if they work like horses—so I know. Now get hold of this poor kid and bath her and get her to bed.'

Lola was sitting on the bottom of the stairs, wailing and disconsolate.

'I want Brownie,' she wept. 'I want Brownie.'

She put out a hand and clung frantically to the shearer begging:

'Don't go, Clancy. Don't go. I'm so miserable, I'm so lonely and frightened and cold.'

Next morning Mrs. Lovell and Lola had a talk. It was the only talk they ever had that was shorn of all mother to daughter trimmings. It was quite a brutal little conversation, Mrs. Lovell began it by asking Lola if she had any desire to do anything decent with her life. Lola said, what was the use? Mrs. Lovell said that she had apparently been mistaken in her daughter. She had hoped for a decent life for her. That was why she had made sacrifices to send her to expensive schools. She had wanted her to meet the right people, become educated for a good job (private secretary, doctor's receptionist...), and in the long run marry someone who would provide her with all the things that Lola's father had never provided for Lola's mother, etc., etc. However, it now seemed that all maternal sacrifice had been in vain; Lola must just be bad like her father.

'That's it, I'm bad,' said Lola.

Mrs. Lovell flared into impatience at this carefully calculated insolence.

'Well, I don't advise you to be too bad while you're under sixteen and still in my care,' she concluded, 'because I'd just as soon put you in a home for uncontrollable girls as

44

look at you. When you're sixteen I wash my hands of you. You can please yourself what you do.'

'I'll keep you up to that,' said Lola.

Then her mother hit her across the face and threw herself down on the bed sobbing.

'What's wrong with you, Lola?' she cried. 'I look at you and wonder what goes on in that mean little inside of yours, and I just don't know. I don't know you at all.'

'Why should you?' thought Lola. She felt a little sorry for the woman sobbing on the bed, but she could not be bothered with talking to her. It flashed through her mind that she could say: 'I waited alone all the years of my childhood for you to come and get to know me,' but she decided it would be pointless now; and at any rate it might give her mother the satisfaction of thinking that she had been hurt. And had she been hurt? She did not know herself. She turned away from her mother and looked out of the window.

The woman who had picked up Brownie was a prostitute called Jan. Or rather she called herself Jan, but that has become a popular name in the profession of late years. Her name could quite possibly have been Ethel or Gwen. In common with most prostitutes, she had a pathetic story. Hers was that she was the daughter of a wealthy family in Sydney and had been well educated; but having had her face badly smashed around in a car accident she had decided not to care any more, and had apparently chosen prostitution as a means of going to waste which involved the least work and the most free drinks. She stuck to her story with a wealth of detail and it is certain that she spoke well when she so desired. Apart from that she was a big, sloppy woman in her early thirties and looking older, with a badly broken nose and a collection of angry-looking scars along her left jaw.

When she and Brownie awoke it was already early afternoon and they were both still a little drunk.

'No point in you going back to your ship today, love,' said Jan. So they repaired to the 'Grand' to pull themselves together with whisky and soda. Then they went out for a hamburger and came back for some solid drinking. Brownie being out of money, Jan paid. He dragged himself back on board the next morning and was not even logged. His mates had covered up for him, feeling that every deck boy is entitled to one bender on a prostitute's money.

'It's part of your education,' said the bosun.

She used to wait for him at the dock gate after that and he found himself the recipient of much ribald congratulation.

'How's our deck boy?' said his older shipmates. 'He's got a whore keeping him.'

Brownie felt very big. He only regretted that he frequently found Jan so very repulsive.

The next time the *Dalton* got into Brisbane she gave him a watch. However, some of her professional colleagues told him that it had been stolen from one of her customers, so Brownie, always a fair-minded lad, at least where his own sex was concerned, made her return it. Frantically she maintained that she loved him, and twice she infected him with the least dignified of parasites—lice. This caused so much merriment amongst his shipmates to whom he went for advice (and some very macabre advice was forthcoming)

46

that he made a great joke of it also, though secretly he was disgusted and horrified to the very depths of his adolescent puritanical soul. The cleansing process almost caused him to vomit, nevertheless it had to be. Setting aside such jocular suggestions as castration and cauterization, he decided upon insecticide, and being too shy to walk into a chemist and demand blue ointment he performed the purification with Mortein plus. It is one hundred per cent effective, but has the one disadvantage that it removes anything up to about three layers of skin along with the parasites. So much for the first time. On the second occasion that he found himself infected he was more than a little annoyed.

'She sure seems to be the careless type,' said the bosun. 'Don't you find it a bit off putting?'

Brownie did, and the next time that he and Jan took to bed he pleaded alcohol and went to sleep. When he woke up he dressed straight away, took his shoes under his arm and sneaked out. Apparently Jan never forgave the slight to her professional pride, for when he was back in Brisbane a couple of months later she came down to the ship all friendliness and relatively spruce looking: 'If Brownie would give her a couple of quid for a drink,' she said, 'and a quid for the hotel room, she would fix everything and meet him at the dock gates that evening.'

Brownie, on whom the celibate life had been weighing heavily, gave her the money and that was the last he saw of her for many a long day. From then on he ignored women till they became a matter of utmost physical necessity, and all the time he kept on looking for Lola.

*

He found her at last in Melbourne on a wet August day about twelve months after he went to sea. It was pay-day and he was in the 'Havana' wine lounge getting drunk. It was his practice to get drunk on payday; and as he had a grown man's capacity and a deck boy's pay, he drank wine, which was cheaper and quicker. And then he saw her. The 'Havana' was in a basement and Lola came down the stairs with a big, wide-shouldered girl whose hair was dyed an unfortunate shade of red, and they sat at a table near the wall and ordered a bottle of dry sherry.

Coming in they had not seen Brownie, who was in a corner by the bar, and now they sat with their backs to him. Brownie's first reaction was that it could not be Lola. She looked terrible; half starved and sick and grubby and wretched, and she had blonded her hair, which did not suit her, and it was going black along the parting.

'God,' he thought, as he made his way between the tables, 'what have they done to her?'

Now he was standing behind her and he put his hand on her shoulder and said:

'Do you mind if I join you girls?'

She turned and looked into his face, and immediately she stood up and he took her in his arms. She was weeping and laughing and exclaiming all at once:

'Oh, God, Brownie, it can't be you, it can't be you. Oh, Brownie, Brownie, darling.' And then to the other girl, 'Kath, this is Brownie.'

'Hell, I've heard plenty about you,' said Kath.

Lola moved around to the wall side of the table, where the seating was a long settle-type bench covered in red velvet and running the length of the room. Brownie moved in beside her and they sat very close, holding hands. Kath said:

'Look, I think I'll go over and collect your bottle, otherwise some thirsty bum will whizz it off.'

When she came back Lola introduced her:

'This is my girl friend Kath Thomson.'

Brownie smiled politely and surveyed her with distaste. She was the type he particularly disliked, big and hard-faced, with square hands like a man.

'How did you get down this far?' he asked Lola.

'I followed the fleet,' said Lola, which Kath seemed to think extremely funny.

'Not Pussas, I hope,' said Brownie.

'Pussas! We wouldn't have them on our mind,' said Kath.

Lola leaned one arm on his shoulder and sipped her sherry with her body pressed against his.

'Are you a big merchant-service sailor now?' she asked and he heard with delight that the sing song had not quite gone from her voice.

'That's right.'

'You're just about Captain now, I suppose.'

'In two months time I'll be a bucko.'

'J.C. a bloody deck boy,' said Kath. 'I thought you were older.'

'He's old enough to take care of me, aren't you, Brownie?' said Lola. 'Look I'm real warm now.' She wriggled happily in his arm. 'That's the first time I've been warm since I came to this lousy hole.'

49

It was small wonder that she was not finding the Melbourne winter very snug, for she was most unsuitably dressed for it in a narrow black skirt of a very light woollen material and a not very fresh-looking embroidered blouse, with a draw string through the neck. She wore the drawstring loose, and quite an amount of breast was disclosed. Over this she wore a fawn duffle jacket with no hood. It was somewhat too large for her, but it was a good warm jacket; however, in a Melbourne winter one warm garment is no more than a daisy in a bull's mouth. The ensemble was finished off with bare legs and ankle-strap shoes, and a huge shoulder-strap bag of black patent leather with a plastic clasp that was vaguely heraldic.

'I'll look after you and keep you warm too,' said Brownie, 'if you still want me.'

'Oh, Brownie,' she put down her glass and looked at him in astonishment.

'Why wouldn't I still want you? Haven't you always been the only one I ever loved?'

'Yes,' said Kath, 'she's always talking about Brownie.' She poured out another drink all round.

'Have another drink on the happy occasion,' she said.

Brownie looked down into his glass.

'I don't need it now,' he said.

'If you two want to go off to bed or somewhere, don't mind me,' said Kath. Brownie looked at Lola.

'What about a meal—it's nearly five o'clock? You too, Kath,' he added in the tone of voice which means 'accept if you dare.'

'I'm not leaving all this lovely liquor,' declared Kath. 'Now run along, kiddies, and be happy.'

Lola hesitated.

'How will you get on, Kath, for a meal?' she asked.

Kath eyed three National Servicemen who were drinking at a nearby table.

'If those guys haven't the price of a feed between them,' she said, 'then I'm slipping.'

Out in the street Lola shivered and pulled the duffle jacket around her.

'Food!' she said with glee. 'Wacko! Come on, Brownie. Tonight we eat. Let's go to the "Crown", I want to show you to a few people.'

Seated in the 'Crown', Lola ate her way through chicken soup, steak and oysters, pineapple fritters and finished off with coffee and toast. She seemed to know every second girl in the place and hailed them all excitedly, telling them all: 'This is Brownie!' And everyone seemed to have heard of him.

As she ate, her face lost its pinched and exhausted look and Brownie became aware that she had developed a certain head-turning quality—whether it was the long-legged, stilt-heeled walk, or the upthrusting breasts, or the sluttish-looking mop of hair, or a combination of all these, he did not know, but he began to feel great pride in his rakish-looking little love as she sat there drinking her coffee and smoking a cigarette. He reached out across the clutter of cups and plates and took her hand between his:

'Have you got somewhere to take me, honey?' he asked. She laughed and patted his cheek.

'Naturally, Brownie,' she said. 'You don't have to come courting. We settled all that under the frangipani trees on the banks of the Burnett River, remember?'

She stood up, put the strap of her bag over her shoulder, turned the collar of her coat up around her face, and put her hands deep in the pockets.

'Follow me, sailor!' she said.

Her room was at the top of a house in a terrace in a back street in St. Kilda, and it was the room that Brownie might have expected—small and mean, with damp on the walls and clothes on the floor and the bed unmade. Lola closed the door and leaned against it, facing him, and he saw now that there were tears in her eyes.

'Oh, Brownie,' she said, 'I know it's terrible and I know I look dreadful, but I've been so sick, and maybe I haven't always done the right thing; but, Brownie, I loved you, I loved you all the time.'

Brownie looked at her, at the thinness of her face and the hollows around her neck, at the streaky blonde hair and the nicotine stains on her fingers.

'God!' he thought, 'she looks as though she's been starving.'

'Brownie, say you still want me. For God's sake say you still want me.'

'I still want you,' he said. 'I want you and love you more than I ever did before in all my life.'

It was midnight. Lola and Brownie had been down the street to buy hamburgers and coke at the all-night hamburger bar at the Junction and now they were back warm and contented in bed. Lola munched her hamburger, curled up in Brownie's arm, her head resting on his shoulder.

'Wouldn't it be good,' she said, 'to be a cat and just spend your life eating and sleeping and making love?'

'Some cats find the alleys a bit cold at times,' said Brownie.

'I believe you, Brownie. Believe me boy, I believe you.'

'Darling, where were you working?'

'Well really I'm not working anywhere just now.'

'What work do you do, darling?'

'Last job I was a waitress. I was in a big place in Collins Street but I got two days notice when the 'flu was coming on me. "You look bad," the Manageress said. I could see she didn't want to give me sick pay so she was giving me orders to balls me up all day and then in the end she said I was insolent.'

'Were you?' he laughed in the darkness and tightened his arms around her body.

'Of course I was.' She laughed too. 'So in the end she told me "take two days notice", and I said "pay me off now, I'll be too sick to work in your lousy drum by tomorrow".'

'How long ago was that, love?'

'Two weeks ago—yesterday was the first day I was up and then I only went out for some rolls and butter and that, and I felt so sick I went back to bed again.'

'Who looked after you—got your meals and that?'

'Teddy Langley used to give me tea and toast in the mornings, and sometimes, nearly every night, Kath would bring me a pie, or fish and chips or something, and she'd heat them on Teddy Langley's gas ring. A few times, though,

53

she went off with some guy or got so rotten she couldn't come.' Lola laughed. 'Once she brought a soldier up here and we had crayfish and beer and all, and the beer sent me to sleep, and when I woke up Kath and the soldier were both in with me, both naked as the day they were born, and the soldier started to go the grope on me, so I woke Kath and said "Do your own dirty work".'

'Very funny,' said Brownie puritanically. 'I don't like Kath.'

'Oh, Brownie, don't be hard to get on with—we all have to live the best we can, and she's a good friend.'

'Sounds like it.'

'Well, she fed me when I was sick and got the doctor when I was delirious.'

'Gee, darling, I didn't know you were that sick.'

'I wasn't too bad, sweetheart. Just I don't seem to have any resistance to colds. Anyway, the doctor prescribed penicillin. It's free medicine you know, and after that I got on fine.'

'You're looking skinny though, darling. Like you haven't had anything solid to eat for a long time.'

'I've got by all right.'

'What were you going to do tonight if I hadn't met you?'

'Like Kath said—pick up a couple of guys to take us to dinner and then maybe go on to the Troc.'

'And then?'

'And then what?'

'That's what I'm asking you!'

'Oh, Brownie darling,' her voice was beseeching now, 'life's so sad most of the time, and we might as well try and enjoy ourselves while we can. If you could only know how cold and lonely and miserable and frightened I've been most of the time.'

'Shush, darling,' he patted her back gently, reassuring a child. 'It doesn't matter. I've been no lilywhite myself. Nothing's changed between you and me. Nothing's changed at all. We'll be all right now; but we must keep together from now on.'

She began to sob with her head against his shoulder and after a while she fell asleep.

They arranged to meet at six-thirty the next evening, after Brownie finished work. Brownie arrived on the steps of Flinders Street Station at six o'clock and at half-past six she was not there. She had not arrived by seven so he caught a taxi down to St. Kilda. He was almost sick with disappointment and apprehension. 'If I find her and Kath drinking with a couple of Nashos it will just serve me right,' he told himself.

But what he found was Lola standing at the doorway arguing with her landlady. The landlady looked irate and Lola looked rueful, but when she saw Brownie she began laughing in a mixture of relief, hysteria and embarrassment and said:

'Oh, Brownie, isn't this awful? I was praying you'd come. This old vulture bailed me up just as I was going out, and she says she is going to get the police and turn me in for insufficient lawful if I don't pay the rent. And I haven't any money.'

Brownie took charge of the situation.

55

'What are you doing to my girl?' he asked the landlady.

'Your girl and everyone else's,' said the landlady.

Brownie hoped he did not flinch outwardly and he went on courageously enough:

'How much is owing to you?'

'Four weeks at thirty shillings a week and ten shillings for gas and electricity.'

'Don't pay the old bitch a penny,' said Lola. 'Threatening to get me vagged! I kept trying to tell her that if she'd only let me go meet you you'd help me.'

'I've heard that one before,' said the landlady. She suddenly switched the attack to Brownie. 'You look the type she'd get in tow.'

Brownie put his hand in his pocket and brought out £2.

'Here's a couple of quid off it,' he said. 'Now let me have that suit-case.'

The landlady took the money and remained where she was, arms folded. 'Are you going to stand like Napoleon on St. Helena all night?' asked Lola. 'Or can we pack up in peace and get out of your bloody joint?'

So the landlady went away and there was not very much to pack. There were two tight black skirts, both split up the side and broken at the zipper; some black lacy underwear which had been very expensive, but which now looked as though it had been made love to both hard and often; a red polo-necked sweater; the off-the-shoulder blouse and the duffle jacket she had worn the day before; a grubby brassière that smelled of perspiration, Hush and Jicki; a chocolate box containing some costume jewellery (most noticeable being a pair of huge gypsy earrings); some

Helena Rubinstein make-up; one towel with Matson Line stamped on it; a copy of the *Shropshire Lad*; a bottle of Widow Wise's Pills (Ladies end irregularity without delay); and a pair of light blue Sears Roebuck jeans.

'Get into the jeans,' said Brownie.

'Browning darling, where are we going?'

He laughed across at her where she stood by the suit-case. She was dressed as when the landlady attacked her—ankle-strap shoes and a black satin slip. She had draped a long black stole, hand-knitted in wool, around her shoulders for warmth, and she was making a terrible job of the packing.

'Darling,' he said, 'leave it all to me. You need someone to look after you as usual—Lord you're a useless little thing. Just put the things you need for the night in your handbag' (Lola promptly tipped the make-up and the jewellery into the shoulder-strap bag) 'and get into your jeans and do what you're told like a good little girl. Have you got any flat shoes?'

A frantic search found a pair of little flat velvet slippers such as matadors wear, under the wardrobe; socks to wear with them this cold night were not forthcoming, and then Teddy Langley, coming in to invite them for a farewell drink, offered a pair of navy blue two-way stretch. Lola introduced Brownie with the usual formula:

'Teddy this is Brownie that I was always talking about.' Then she put on the socks and turned them under at the heel.

'So much more comfortable than taking in the slack at the toes,' she told them.

They had the drink with Teddy and were ready to go. At the last moment Teddy took his football supporter's cap from his pocket and set it on her head. It was a knitted cap with a pom-pom, white and black, for Teddy was a Collingwood supporter by religious conviction.

'There you are you one-eyed Demon fan,' he said. 'I suppose it'll kill you to wear it, but you have to keep dry; you've been very sick.'

'Can you grab a cab while I get the case downstairs?' said Brownie, who did not much care for it when Lola woke the protective instinct in other males. Teddy got the cab and Brownie carried her case. Lola left in style.

'Wacko! Who would have thought that I'd drive away in a taxi?' she said. 'Now, Brownie, what gives with you, where are we going?'

But he wouldn't tell her till they got out at Flinders Street Station and cloaked her suit-case in the baggage-room.

'Now look, Lola,' he said. 'Come and eat and I'll tell you what I'm going to do. You'll have to be careful and do everything I say because it's a risk, but it's our only chance to be together—O.K.?'

She nodded at him like a docile child.

'You're looking after me now,' she said.

So, sitting in the Greek's over spaghetti and meat balls, he told her:

'Look, Lola, I'll have to get you in off the street some-where tonight or you'll be vagged; and I haven't got much money left so I'm taking you down on the ship.'

Lola looked eager.

'I'll like that,' she said.

'It's not that much,' he warned her. 'Nothing like parties on ships and so on. We've been laid up for six weeks. I suppose you've heard the miners are on strike?'

Lola had heard it vaguely.

'Well, the ships are tied up for lack of coal, or the shipping companies are saying they have no coal, that way they make the miners look bastards, and on my ship they've only kept me and the bosun working by. I'll try and get you on board for tonight and maybe tomorrow you can get a job somewhere, just to keep you going till next pay-day—that is, if you're well enough, darling. The bosun is living in a pub up on shore. He comes down in the morning and puts me on the shake but I'll have you out of the way by then. Want to give it a go?'

'O.K. Let's go.'

He zipped her bag inside his leather jacket, turned her coat collar up around her face and pushed her hair under the stocking cap. Sitting in the back of the taxi, trying to look like another deck boy, she drove through the wharf gates.

Once on the ship Brownie had to light a kerosene lantern to take her forward, for without coal the ship was without electricity. She lay a lifeless thing, cold, her woodwork and bulkheads damp to the touch, but Lola went below joyfully.

'Brownie,' she said, 'this is wonderful.' She looked around the lantern-lit cabin and sat down on the bottom bunk.

'Isn't it silent,' she said, 'right down here? I feel like we are at the bottom of a well, walled away from everything. At last I feel like nothing can harm us.'

Brownie sat beside her and put his arms around her.

'I'd like to wall you away from everything,' he said, 'and love you and love you hard for a hundred years.'

As events fell out Lola did not have to slip ashore early in the morning, for both she and Brownie overslept and they woke to find the bosun standing over them. He called Brownie outside and said:

'You know what the Union says about women on board. Did you both pass out with the grog or something?'

Brownie, shivering in his jeans and rubbing the sleep out of his eyes, knew that the bosun was trying to provide him with a loophole, but somehow he could not take it.

'No,' he said, 'that's my girl. The one the police took away from me. I just found her again last night.'

'She looks like she's come a long way from the old home town,' said the bosun.

'I suppose so.'

'Where did you pick her up again?'

'What's it to you?'

'O.K. O.K. Just be careful she doesn't give you a dose or something.'

'She's not like that.'

'Of course not,' the bosun hastened to agree; he could not forbear to add, however, that it was a well-known fact that the worst dose of all was the dose you got from a virgin.

'She's been very sick with 'flu,' said Brownie, 'and she hasn't any money.'

'No job of course?'

'No job.'

60

Outside the Melbourne rain rattled on the deck.

'I wouldn't put a dog out in this,' said the bosun. 'You'd better put her in my cabin; it's supposed to be locked.' He handed Brownie the key.

'Mind you, if you're caught, I know nothing about it at all. Only for a couple of days it is, till you find her somewhere else and she gets a chance to pull round.'

Lola stayed in the bosun's cabin a fortnight, for the 'flu, half arrested by insufficient penicillin, and encouraged by cold and sherry and intensive love-making, returned in virulent strength, and for a week she scarcely left her bunk. For the first couple of days she was very feverish: she lay shivering and sneezing while Brownie and the bosun ran her relays of hot tea and Aspros, lemon drinks and hot rum and lemon—this last was a sovereign cure of the bosun's dear old mother back in Limehouse, and they poured it into Lola till she was in danger of D.T.'s, a side effect of the cure that had never distressed the bosun's dear old mother.

'You really shouldn't be sleeping with her,' he said on the third day when he had taken her temperature with the thermometer burgled from the second mate's cabin.

'Are you going all moral on us?' asked Lola.

She was sitting up clad in a black satin slip and a ship's blanket, and the general effect was both cheerful and cheeky despite the temperature. 'Get your lunch into you and give less slack,' said the bosun.

He had gone ashore to personally supervise the cutting of the chicken sandwiches she said she wanted, and now he stood watching her eat, his face (and it was a grim old face even as bosuns go) wreathed in a look of imbecile doting.

61

Lola reached out and patted his hand.

'Gee, you're good to me,' she said.

'Why shouldn't I sleep with her,' said Brownie brusquely. He was finding the bosun, in his role of kindly old guide, confidant, philosopher and friend, a bit much.

'Good grief, the girl's got a temperature of 101, it hasn't gone down for days.' The bosun's voice was one long cadence of righteous indignation. 'It's no time for love-making. You could give her pneumonia.'

'Is that all?' said Lola. 'I thought you were going to say "you could give her a baby!"'

'There is that too,' said the bosun, 'but that's his blue. Now I'm going to the galley to get your coffee, and I want to see every bit of your lunch gone when I come back.'

'What a fatherly old soul he turned out to be,' said Brownie. 'I'm impressed. "You shouldn't really be sleeping with her",' he mocked the bosun's tone of concern. 'AAAAH—he'd be up you like a rat up a drain-pipe, given the chance.'

Lola laughed and blew him a kiss.

'Don't blow kisses with your mouth full of chicken sandwich.'

'Come on, Brownie darling, be gruntled.'

Brownie grinned, but he stuck to his point. He would watch the bosun, he said, and while he was on the subject would Lola please don a jumper or the duffle jacket over the black satin slip next time that she had her temperature taken. 'That dockside waif act,' he said, 'might be very romantic to shore types, but it only meant the one thing where sailors were concerned.'

The next morning her temperature was almost normal and the bosun decided she could get up for a while, provided she was wrapped up warm.

A ship docked in Melbourne in winter is not the ideal place for a convalescent, and when, added to the damp and emptiness, there is the fact that there is neither light nor heating for the length and breadth of the ship, it is surprising that Lola did not go down with the pneumonia that the bosun predicted. But she was too happy to be ill. Her day began at about ten in the morning. Before that she was locked securely in the cabin for the mate came down early to give Brownie and the bosun detail for the day. The mate out of the way, she would appear wearing jeans and a couple of Brownie's jumpers for warmth, full makeup, the gold cartwheel earrings and the hair pulled on the top of the head. Then she would prepare morning smoko. She liked the galley where the primus stove provided to heat Brownie's food made the atmosphere pleasantly oppressive and warm as the day went on. She would sit there for hours, frying the sausages and tomatoes or heating the fish and chips or sometimes trying a little adventurous cooking. Her masterpiece was caramel, made by boiling a tin of condensed milk till the contents were yellow and syrupy. She and Brownie loved it. The bosun was twenty years older and not so keen. She darned all their socks and read several books in the ship's library. It puzzled her a little that seamen, with all the wonders of the world just a voyage away, in a manner of speaking, should take such an interest in the impossible marvels of the more lurid type of historical fiction—what Brownie called 'lusty busties'.

'Wouldn't you think they would read Joseph Conrad?' said Lola innocently. She had just discovered Conrad, and had decided he was her favourite author.

'Who's he?' asked Brownie.

Lola explained. Brownie snorted. He said that if Joseph Conrad was a sailor he should have known better than to go writing about the sea—and who wanted to read about the sea anyway.

'I do,' said Lola.

'You're an idiot,' said Brownie with affection.

Her favourite time was in the evening when the deserted docks were silent and the bosun had gone ashore, and she and Brownie sat with the primus brewing up endless cups of coffee, while they talked about what they were going to do, and how they were never going to be parted again, and all the adventures that would befall them when Brownie was captain of his own trading schooner. Sometimes they were invited by a couple of Brownie's deck-boy friends, and then he was very proud. These boys had girl friends, but he was the only one in his crowd actually living with a woman—and installed on the ship into the bargain. He felt this called for a little showing off. So they had a couple of very enjoyable parties. They bought some spring rolls and beer, and the other two deck-boys brought a girl and a bottle of wine apiece, and there was a Jamaican with a portable record player and some Scotch, and one of the toughest old bats around the Melbourne waterfront whom he treated with almost unbelievable courtesy. They crowded into the bosun's cabin with the music going full blast. They sang; they told stories; they boasted of their encounters with

64

the police—with the exception of the Jamaican's woman, who did not want to put amateurs out of countenance. None of the women were working, and none of them had really enough to eat or enough clothes to keep them warm, but they sat there in their tight skirts, drinking out of the bottle and making love to their men, and had any officious, interfering welfare worker tried to drag them away to the well-lit, well-run, well-fed suburbs on the other side of the river they would have fought like tiger-cats.

It was on the next pay-day (all Australian seamen are paid about the first and the fifteenth of the month) that the vice squad swooped. There had been rumours of a social life much too enjoyable for sailors going on in these empty docks; and then two fourteen-year-olds had been picked up selling themselves at ten shillings the throw to the crew of an American tanker. The police took them home and told their parents, who had thought they were at basket-ball, and the next day they were back again at their price-cutting. They had to be taken in. And then the Jamaican and two friends, also Jamaican, who had taken a flatlette in St. Kilda, and who had thought they were sheltering three charming and cultured young ladies, refreshingly free from racial prejudice, found, simple fellows, when they came home from wielding their paint-brushes and chipping hammers, that they were on a charge of having allowed the premises to be used for purposes of prostitution.

And so, on the first of September, the wharves echoed to the rumble of police cars and the shrieks of harlots—skilled and semi-skilled.

The *Dalton* lying stodgy and dark by the wharf escaped all suspicion, but later that night, when all the hubbub had died down, Brownie, Lola and the bosun took counsel over a cup of coffee.

'It's been fun,' said Lola, 'but it's time I got a job.'

Early next morning Brownie fetched a taxi from the dock gates and got her safely off the ship. With her skirt pressed, a new black jumper, gift of the bosun, and a pair of stockings, Brownie's contribution, she was sufficiently tidied up to land a drink waitress's job; and when the strike ended and the *Dalton* sailed for Sydney, a week later, she had quite a little nest egg saved up out of tips—more than enough for her train fare to Sydney.

In Sydney she and Brownie had a glorious week doing the Cross, which culminated in a rather uncomfortable little interview with a policeman outside Bert's milk bar; after which Lola, very wisely, caught the train up to Brisbane, where she waited for Brownie, who arrived two days later.

In Brisbane, Brownie paid off. He was now out of his deck-boy's time and he had his wages and thirty pounds accumulated time. They decided that Lola should not get a job till the thirty pounds were gone and Brownie had picked another ship. So they took a room in Spring Hill and proceeded to spend Brownie's fortune. It was a terrible room in a frightful old house, but there was a frangipani tree bursting into flower outside the window and Lola brought a Chinese lantern to hang over the electric light bulb, and a secondhand shawl of Jap silk to drape across the bed, and Brownie said the effect was fabulous. He bought her a new black skirt (skin tight of course), and a pair of gold matador

66

pants (also skin tight). These last Lola usually wore with a shirt of Brownie's, which he had outgrown. With the sleeves rolled up and the buttons undone to the waist, it was very sharp, and the girl in the next room said she had just the belt to set it off. She would sell it to Lola for 2/6. It was a good four inches wide, that belt, and studded all over with imitation American dollars.

'I'm getting too fat for it love,' said the girl in the next room. 'It's the frigging grog. It's just right for you.'

Thus dressed, and with a rich gentleman friend with thirty pounds in his pocket to pay her rent, Lola was qualified to sally out and give cheek to the police whenever she met them. She met them first one evening in Wickham Terrace. She and Brownie had just got out of bed (and looked like it) and were wandering along looking for somewhere to have a steak to keep up their strength. The police sprung them from a doorway, and, of course, separated their quarry before they started questioning. Luckily, Brownie and Lola (wise since their brush with Bumper) had rehearsed for just such an occasion. So Lola decided to play them along a little.

'You're a stranger here aren't you?' said her policeman.

'Yes.'

'Are you from Sydney?'

'Yes.'

'What's your name?'

'Confidentially, Officer, I'm Kate Leigh without her fur.'

'Don't get cheeky. What's your name?'

'Lola Hansen.'

'Are you working?'

'No.'

'Don't you think you'd better get a job?'

'No.'

'Well I think you'd better.'

'O.K., Officer—you can take it up with my husband, he doesn't believe in married women working.'

'Is that bodgie your husband?'

'He's a seaman, registered at the pick-up, and he's got money in the bank. You can't touch him.' And diving into the shoulder-strap bag which was, as usual, swinging bulging in one hand, and coming forth in triumph with a bank book, 'Here's identification.' The account had been made out jointly in the names of Lola Mary Hansen and Goran Olaf Hansen and it still contained twenty-five pounds. Triumph! Complete triumph! Lola and Brownie felt almost sorry for the police; and the police, who were just ordinary beat-sloggers and had not achieved the misanthropy necessary to making a success of the vice squad, felt almost sorry for Brownie and Lola.

Where they lived everyone considered that Lola had been tremendously witty in this little brush with the Force. She began to feel that she should be very pleased with herself.

'But give them no cheek, Darl, when you've got no dough in the kick,' said the girl from the next room, who was a very wise girl indeed.

So for a few weeks Lola and Brownie had a wonderful time. They got up when they liked, went dancing, drinking and eating when they liked, and Brownie kept saying that he really should go down to the pick-up and see if there were some short-run ships on the roster. But somehow it seemed too hard to face the fact that all this must come to an end; and the atmosphere where they lived was very matey, idle and relaxing. Nobody worked and everybody seemed to get by all right. There were two Norwegians who had paid off from the Tangalooma whaling station with two thousand pounds apiece and were being helped to spend it by every good-time Charlie in Spring Hill—black, white or brindle. They threw parties every night to which all were welcome. There was a blonde called Edna who went out every evening baby-sitting, she said; and the girl whose figure had gone to the grog. Her name was Dawn, and she was very scornful of Edna's baby-sitting. Dawn was a prostitute, straight out, and said so—no baby-sitting alibi for her. In the room on the other side of Brownie and Lola there were three Siamese University students, who were concentrating their studies on the rowdier side of Australian social life. And then there was the landlady who was fat, bleary and alcoholic, but very kind and easy going, and not prone to the terrible little 'Please switch off the light' and 'Please keep the bathroom clean' notes to which her profession is so addicted. Last of all was her lover, Snow—a terrible, red-eyed, weedy seventeen-year-old, who was in a chronic state of stomach upset because he could not keep up with her in the drinking. His duties were light (depending how you looked at it), consisting as they did of making a pretence of cleaning up the yard and making love to the landlady regularly every morning between nine and ten.

'I'm never available then, love,' she told Lola, 'because that's when me and Snow have the business.'

She was twenty years older than Snow and at least four stone heavier, as well as smelling most nose-searingly of gin: it was apparent that Snow found his sexual duties somewhat onerous, for he always emerged at ten o'clock in a raging bad temper, and kicked the landlady's cat as though he envied it its castration. Then he would take a heavily disinfected bath. Brownie called him the Solyptol kid!

By the end of October, Brownie was down to his last ten shillings, and the sea was staring him in the face. He said as much to Lief, the dark Norwegian, who was sitting on his bed late one afternoon holding his head in his hands.

'Yes,' said Lief. 'Me, I go back to sea too. Is clean there, away from all this shit. No good drinking all the time.'

He glanced across at Arne, the blond Norwegian, who was lying in a heap in a corner, sleeping with his head on a packet of prawns.

'I don't like leaving Lola,' said Brownie.

Lief began to weep. He said he knew how it was. He left a little girl in Norway. Ah, such a good little girl. Best little girl in Bergen. He was going to get a ship and sail back to her tomorrow. Brownie must not leave Lola. No, no. The Hansens and the Johannsens must stick together. He must insist that Brownie take this fiver and stay a little longer. They would all go down to the 'Grand' now and have a drink. Better still they would go and get a supply of schnapps. They would have another party on the spot. Arne must be woken so that he could play the accordion. No sooner said than done. Brownie went off with the fiver and bought the liquor, Lief poured water over Arne's head till he woke, and by seven o'clock the party was in full swing.

At about nine o'clock Lola and Brownie volunteered to go and buy some beer (this time the Siamese put up the money). This was the unluckiest thing they did in many a long day, for when the beer had been bought and dispatched in a taxi with Utai, Lola, who was just drunk enough to be capricious, decided that she would like to stay at the 'Grand' for a couple of drinks. She wanted to see a couple of girls. The police picked them up at a quarter to ten, and this time they had only 2/6 on them.

Brownie was fined for drinking while under age and bound over not to see Lola or try to contact her for twelve months: Lola was put into Jacaranda Flats Girls' Corrective School. Brownie decided to fill in the twelve months by going overseas, and the day Lola went into Jacaranda Flats he sailed for Stockholm on a Swedish tanker.

By November Lola knew now for certain that she was pregnant, which cheered her considerably, though her mother, who came to see her regularly, obviously thought that this was the worst thing that could have happened.

'It's not as though, Lola,' she said, 'I wouldn't give consent for you to marry the great hobbledehoy—I'm past caring now; but you saw how his mother behaved about you, coming into court and breathing fire about what a harlot you were. If either of you expect *her* consent you're just putting yourself in the way of needless humiliation, and, I don't know about you, but I've had all the humiliation I can stand.'

'I feel for you,' said Lola.

Then she said: 'I'm sorry, Mum,' for she remembered that when she left Brisbane shortly after her sixteenth birthday her mother had wept bitterly, and Lola had been dressed like a fashion plate and acting as though the world were at her feet. She had had an American on a Pioneer boat to look after her then, and her mother had not stopped her going. She had merely said:

'I just don't seem to succeed with you however I try; but if you strike trouble wire for money to come home.'

But her mother had told the Welfare that she was uncontrollable and that she should be put in a home for twelve months—it would give her a chance to learn an interesting trade. Without her mother's betrayal she would probably only have got three months for a first vag. She had her mother to thank for an extra nine months' claustrophobic hell while every fibre of her body and soul cried out for the freedom of the streets.

The vocational guidance officer had asked her would she like to take up dressmaking, or a commercial course, or nursing or hairdressing or weaving. Lola had said she would like to learn the guitar and the vocational guidance officer had given her a long spiel about how she should try to break away from the rock and roll crowd, and Lola had not listened. She decided he was a fool and she was right. Finally, to pacify him, she took to thumping away dispiritedly at a typewriter.

'It may come in handy some day,' she told the girl in the next seat. 'When I'm writing my book: "Bastards I have known."'

'What's it going to be about—men?'

'Men and social workers.'

'Shit! Some bastardry,' said the girl in the next seat.

And then in January came the riot. It was a famous riot, long remembered in the annals of delinquency, and Lola never forgot it in all her life. For when the glorious hysteria and violence was over, and the laundry windows were broken and the bedding burned in dormitory A, and the Matron had had her false teeth smashed by big Daff from the 'Gabba, and the police had been called in and order almost restored, Lola found she was lying on a strip of torn lawn, and she had a black eye and a broken wrist and she was having a very messy miscarriage. Big Daff sat down beside her, exhausted, and took her head in her lap.

'Shit! you're a mess, kid,' she said. 'You can go. I'll give you that; but you have to spot too much weight. You're too titchy to blue on.'

'What happens now?' whispered Lola and then fainted clean away.

'Now,' answered Daff, watching a party of police-women and attendants approach, 'Now we pay very dearly for Horrorhead's false tats. Look what you've done to my friend,' she told the policewomen. 'You frigging great animals.'

That was the end of all efforts to teach Lola Lovell a useful trade. They sent her to a convalescent home and patched her up, and then she came back to Jacaranda Flats and sat around dazed and shocked for a few months more. They let her out when she had done nine months because they were sorry for her and because they thought she was hopeless anyway. She was paroled in the care of the famous Mrs. Westbury. The newspapers called her Auntie Westbury, 'the motherly little lady who has been Auntie to two generations of delinquent girls...'

'I always have my girls to live with me,' she told reporters regularly. 'Half the battle is won if you can just show those poor street rambling kids how much better a life a woman can have right in her own home, and how happy you can be instead of chasing out after cheap thrills around the milk bars and places like that.'

She was a beaming little lady with a large motherly bosom and a face like a pretty doll. She welcomed Lola with high tea and a terrifying array of cakes (all home-made by Auntie Westbury's own little plump hands) and the best painted china and many lace d'oyleys.

'They sent me a full report, dear,' she told Lola. 'I have it right here.' She patted her pocket and gave Lola a look like a little bright-eyed bird who is being triumphant over a particularly succulent worm. 'But we're just not going to think about it any more. I'm a great one for my own sex and I always say "it must have been the boy's fault" every time.'

Lola looked at the chocolate cake. Brownie had loved chocolate cake, and she remembered how once they had bought a bag of éclairs and eaten them in the park and fed pieces to the birds. Now she had a vision of him had he been with her now, sitting just across the table from her with a slab of cake in his ugly, gentle hands and the brown curls brushed away from his forehead. How the love and delight in her presence would shine all over his soft honest Scandinavian face. Suddenly she put her head down on the table and burst into a passion of weeping right there amongst Auntie Westbury's loathsome, bloody cream buns.

A few weeks later Brownie received the following letter forwarded on to him from the Australian Consulate in San Francisco:

'Dear Brownie,' it read. 'Please come home and rescue me I am living at above address. They have paroled me into the hands of a most terrible old woman. I am frightened of her. First time in my life I have ever been really truly frightened. Please excuse pencil and incoherence. I am writing this in the dunny in great haste. It is the only place where I can be sure she isn't watching me. The Welfare say I must stay here till I'm eighteen. Oh, Brownie, I would not be able to bear it except that I know that you'll come straightaway. She is a doer of good deeds. Keeps on feeding me up on marmite and wholemeal bread and beautiful food, etc. Says I need building up and I'm not really bad, just need caring for, says to forget everything and I remember you every minute my beautiful, oh my beautiful. She says her own baby girl died and she couldn't have any more so she decided to devote her life to unwanted girls. I want to scream at her "Brownie wants me, Brownie wants me all the time and I want him". She's had a grand old time interfering all these years. Brownie, they took your photo away in the horror chambers and hacked off my hair. She wants to give me a home perm. Says she gives all her girls a home perm and it's wonderful the difference it makes in your outlook. Remember how long and straight my hair was and how you used to rub your face in it? Says she'll help me to get

75

a nice job. She'll help me I can just imagine—nursing or something terrible, I just know. She called in to see Mum the other night. Mum was so pissed she couldn't scratch herself. "That's not your fault, dear," she says. Then she pats me and says, "Poor little thing, I know what it's been like." She knows damn all. She keeps on asking awful questions about you. She asked me did I really like having sex (that's what she calls making love, in an awful smarmy tone of voice), or did I just want to feel that I belonged somewhere. Darling, when I was in the horror chambers I thought of so many things I would write to you when I got the chance, but now all I can think is that I love you and I'm frightened. Please come back straightaway. Lola.'

Poor Lola. Both she and Brownie, used to the Australian coast, had calculated without any knowledge of the length of time it might take for a seaman to be reached on the American coast. Brownie had been trying to get home for a month before he received that letter, and it was another six weeks before he got a tanker out of Galveston.

Back in Australia, Lola waited. She took a job in the cosmetics department of a big city store and she quite enjoyed the work. Aunt Westbury had spoken lovingly of wonderful jobs up the country, of girls of hers who had married thriving dairy farmers and country store-keepers, after having gone to somewhere miles beyond the Black Stump to help look after Mrs. So and So's children, or to milk the cows.

But Lola was firm. She knew she was not shaping as desired and she had lost none of her initial fear of Mrs. Westbury; but to the country she just could not go.

All the time she waited for a letter from Brownie, unaware that the letter he had written within an hour of receiving her address was on its way back to the States, endorsed 'Not known at this address.'

One day Auntie was entertaining one of her favourite girls. 'One of my successes,' she told Lola. 'I want you to meet her. She just couldn't seem to keep out of bad company in the city, and when she went up the country she had nothing except a couple of gay little dresses I made her. Now she has her own home and everything a woman could desire, electric stove and wall to wall carpets, and her husband has his own carrying business. She has to bring her little girl down to the Children's every month. She's a dear little thing; but she's got a hare lip and they're having treatment for it. They always come around here afterwards. They *wouldn't* miss.'

Lola came home from work and the success was still there sitting with her child on her knee in Auntie Westbury's kitchen. The success was called Isobel: she wore a floral dress, a brown shorty coat, and one of the home perms which Auntie so recommended as a morale-booster. Lola looked at the child with pity.

'My Brownie would never have thrown a kid like that,' she thought. 'He may not have his own carrying business, but he'd never throw a poor little gargoyle like that.'

'They've got some marvellous costumes down town,' the success was saying. 'There was one in powder blue' ('get those hips in powder blue,' communed Lola with herself) 'but I thought I'd put the money on some of that rubberized lino for the kitchen.'

'Your home will pay you better dividends,' said Auntie.

Lola poured herself a cup of tea and wondered what there was about such pronouncements that made her want to shout 'Shit' at the top of her voice.

'How do you like the chocolate cake?' asked Auntie. 'Isobel made it for me. She's a wonderful cook. She's got a marvellous stove. Thermostatically controlled.'

Lola lifted one eyebrow to indicate that thermostatically controlled stoves left her unmoved.

'We're trying to get Lola interested in cooking,' Auntie went on, 'but so far without much result.'

'It'll come,' said the success. 'I bet one day I'll come down and you'll be swapping recipes with the best of them.'

'Never,' said Lola with fervour. She went on to say that it must be very tiresome having to tend a kitchen full of bright, shining dishwashing machines, magical stoves, mixmasters, and all the rest of it.

'Well,' said the success, 'it's just that there's something about it that makes every woman worthy of the name just love to do it.' And Auntie went on to say that there was a great satisfaction to the womanly heart in lifting a beautiful chocolate cake out of the oven. Lola drank her tea and looked through the kitchen window. The success and Auntie went on to discuss the success's kitchen garden, which, it appeared, was doing 'real well,' but was much plagued by the snails, so the success was going to get a couple of those, what do they call them? Muscovy ducks to eat them up. And the success was knitting harelip a lovely fair-isle jumper, and Auntie became quite animated at the mention of fair-isle. On and on it went. All the old and beautiful arts of cooking and sewing and making a home swamped in a sea of banality that was too cloying to be quite real, even taking into account the two protagonists. It was unbelievable. It sounded like a programme to teach New Australian women English. Lola fought down a desire to laugh hysterically, or else to say,

'Oh, Stephanie. They are Muscovy ducks. They are not Muscovy ducks, Stephanie. The ducks are called Muscovy ducks.'

It was quite obvious that they were talking at her. This is perhaps the meanest of all female tricks, because if those on the receiving end of all the propaganda and innuendo dare to protest they immediately face a charge of paranoia.

'Why should we be trying to impress you? What makes you think you're so important...?'

'Excuse me, there's the postman,' said Lola.

'Nothing today, love,' said the postman. 'Looks like you'll have to write yourself one.'

Lola tried to smile and then the postman looked at her again. He had delivered letters for thirty years and well knew the face of a woman sick with anxiety.

'I'm expecting a letter from abroad, from America,' she said.

The postie put down his bag.

'There was a letter from America last week,' he said. 'Mrs. Westbury gave it back to me. "No one of that name here," she said.'

'Gawd,' said the success, 'you look like you've seen a ghost.'

Mrs. Westbury had put the tea cups in the sink and Lola, without speaking went across and began to wash them. What was she to do? She had lost. Brownie would think she had gone away without leaving a forwarding address. He would think she did not care. He would not come back. She must go now. She must go to the Shipping Office. What was she doing washing dishes? Like a sleep-walker she drew her hands out of the suds and then she rubbed them on the sides of her skirt.

Now this was a habit of which Auntie had playfully said she would break Lola if it took a million years. Her dear mother, said Auntie, had been a famous trainer of servant girls and every time a girl had been addicted to this serious domestic crime her mother would just say in an admonishing tone 'Ida', or 'Florrie', or 'Jane' or whatever the unfortunate's name might be, and not a girl but was cured completely and lived to be grateful to Auntie Westbury's dear mother. Auntie would perform the same kind of office for Lola, which she did to Lola's unspeakable annoyance. Now she said 'Lola' in the famous tone of voice, with a smile on the little pink face, and at that all hell broke loose. By way of a curtain raiser Lola sent three of Auntie Westbury's best china cups crashing against the wall, and then, with all the fear and anger and hurt and boredom released within her, she was hanging on to the sink and screaming such abuse as can be achieved only by a girl who has been reformed at the taxpayer's expense.

'God! How I hate you, how I hate you,' she was shrieking, 'and your blasted little house and everything about you. I haven't words to tell you how I hate you. You

sent my letter back, I know about it. The postman told me.
Now Brownie will think that I can't be bothered to leave an
address for him to write. You did it on purpose because you
hate me. You hate all girls. You just like to muck people's
lives around. Oh I hate the sight, sound and smell of you.
God! What it's been like here in this cosy little hell hole with
you smacking your lips over stories about girls in brothels
and God knows where, and gloating over the poor bitches
that you've had locked up here'—she extended a shaking
hand towards the heap of smashed china in the corner—
'like the poor God-forsaken bitch that painted that stuff.
Holed up here like something in a trap waiting for her baby
to be born and painting that while she waited. I've thought
of her every time I looked at it. I've never drunk tea out
of it, but I thought I would choke. And then her kid was
born and you persuaded her to let her mother take it. God
that's lovely, that is. You may be proud of that one. Getting
her to pose as the kid's eldest sister and now the kid is
dead "killed in a car crash—perhaps a blessing." Well, my
mother paid a doctor to murder my first kid. Do you think
that's a blessing? And a great frigging woman cop belted
the next one out of me—another blessing I suppose.' Lola
had been screaming all this full voice and now she stopped
for breath, leaning over the sink and weeping and gasping
like one who has been struck a body blow. Indeed her whole
body felt ill with shock, and fear that she might not find
Brownie again.

Auntie Westbury had been watching her fascinated.
The eyes were sparkling, the cheeks pinker, and Lola,
in the midst of all her despair and excitement, saw that

Auntie was really enjoying all this. Somewhere at the back of her mind a civilized gene or two was telling her that she would have given less satisfaction all round if she had carried it off with calm dignity. It was at this moment that Mrs. Westbury chose to step forward and put a hand on her shoulder and say:

'Lola, I was only thinking of your good.'

And then Lola hit her, it was a beauty, fair on the jaw. It did not knock Auntie out because Lola packed very little weight in spite of all Auntie's famous cooking, and Auntie was a solid little woman. She did, however, sit down very suddenly with a strange gasping little sound.

All the time the success sat there nursing her child. She had been watching with interest. Now she sprang to Auntie's assistance, but Lola was obviously through with fisticuffs. She stood nursing the wrist she had broken the night of the riot and feeling it for new damage.

'Relax,' she told the success, and now she was quite rational and calm. 'I've done in my wrist again, I think. I'll do no more damage.'

She turned to the woman in the chair.

'I would advise you,' she said, 'to have that nice cup of tea you always prescribe for others in times of grief and strife, because I am now about to go, and you'll have no one to torture till the Welfare sends someone else, so you'll just have to content yourself with pulling the wings off flies.' She ripped the floral skirt from around her waist. 'Here,' she said in the voice of one returning a borrowed book, 'is the abominable little skirt that you and I had such fun running up on your nice electric machine that sews

82

frontwards and backwards and sidewards and all around the town, and buttonholes, and God knows what other shit. You can stick your little skirt. It's not full enough to be smart and not tight enough to be smart. Of its kind it's a masterpiece.'

She stepped out of the skirt and stood in her blouse and a pair of black briefs.

'I am now,' she announced, 'going to dress myself in a right skirt, pack a few things and leave.'

'I forgive you, Lola,' said Mrs. Westbury, 'but the Welfare will not allow you to leave here.'

'I'm not frightened of the bloody old Welfare,' said Lola, who feared it only a little less than she feared Auntie Westbury, 'and I'd rather go to jail than stay here.'

Suddenly the success, child on hip, confronted her.

'You little tripe hound,' shrieked the success, 'you're going on the streets, aren't you? You ungrateful little bitch, after all that's been done for you you're going to go on the streets.'

Lola looked at her and then she grinned and tapped her on the shoulder with the back of her hand.

'Don't be envious, mate,' she said. 'We can't all go on the streets as you so quaintly put it, and you've got your nice kitchen to make up for it. You know the nice kitchen with the rubber-backed lino and the electric stove with the thermostat and the mixmaster, the thousand-unit fridge, which makes such beaut ice-cream, the Hoover and the washing-machine and the built-in laminex-covered wireless so that you can listen to your serials in the morning and everything.'

Once in town she realized that she was in big trouble. She had a broken wrist, very little money, and nowhere to go. She thought of her mother, but the Welfare would look for her there; besides, she felt she could not run the risk of finding her mother drunk. Tomorrow she would not be able to go back to her job because she would be looked for there. She was even afraid to leave her suit-case at the railway station—policewomen love railway stations—so finally she hid it in an empty house that was falling to pieces up on Gregory Terrace. Then she went in search of Dawn.

Dawn was not to be found, so Lola spent the night crouching beside her case in the empty house, and in the morning she went out to wander around town, feeling feverish and lightheaded with the pain in her wrist and also, though she did not know it, a stiff dose of pleurisy that gave her a pain like a red-hot knife in her left side. She found Dawn that morning by the painstaking method of tracking her from address to address. Dawn had been at four places in nine months and when Lola found her she was still in bed.

'Come in, kid, come in,' she invited, no whit embarrassed by the National Service Trainee customer who still slumbered beside her. He was covered in adolescent acne and smelled to high heaven of port wine. He must have been eighteen to be doing his Nasho's, but he certainly did not look it.

Dawn was all geniality as she hopped out of bed and Lola saw that she had become immense. She pulled a dressing-gown on over her naked body and Lola was surprised to see that she was glistening with sweat.

'Is it hot?' Lola asked, in a voice that sounded to herself to be coming from under layers and layers of cotton wool. 'Gee, I feel as cold as can be.'

Dawn gave a wrench at the top of the dressing-gown to see if she could prevent it from gaping too widely across the bloated obscenity of her breasts, decided to give it up as a bad job and sat down and poured herself a drink. She looked warily at Lola.

'Look, kid,' she said, 'if you're in trouble I haven't got any dough, and I'm not sticking my neck out to get into any trouble with the cops.'

Lola said that she had not been going to ask for money; but she had been going to, and she was considerably disappointed in Dawn, whom she had never seen before in one of her businesslike moods. She did tell as much of her story as she thought necessary, and when it was over Dawn had had two drinks and stopped shaking and was in a more expansive frame of mind.

'Well, you can't go to work, that's for sure,' she said, 'you'd be picked up. And you can't go to hospital to have that wrist set for the same reason, so, what are you going to do? Where's Brownie?'

'He's in the States.'

'Yes, sure.'

'He is, Dawn, no falsing. I've only got to hang out till he comes back and that should be soon.'

'Out of sight out of mind, honey, he won't be back.'

'Look, Dawn, can I camp in with you for a few days till I get to feeling a bit better?'

Dawn thought about it and then gave permission, very grudgingly.

'Remember,' she warned, 'if the cops spring you here, I know nothing and no charity moll capers with my men.'

'I'm not a charity moll, and anyway I feel too sick.'

Dawn said that was all right to say, but it was a well-known fact that anyone who had just come out of Jacaranda Flats would be rairing to go. Lola shook her head wearily.

'I feel too sick,' she repeated, and seated herself in an armchair—the larger of the two which, standing in a corner beside a globeless standard lamp, apparently put the sitting into Dawn's bed-sitting-room.

For the next week she spent most of her time crouched in that chair. She even slept huddled in it, sometimes with an army greatcoat thrown across her, sometimes without. She should by rights have hated it, but she was too stunned with misery to notice anything very much, not even pain nor cold nor hunger. One of Dawn's clients, who claimed to have done two years' medicine, set her wrist. After that it hurt less but it was impossible to get work with one wrist strapped up, so she hung around in a sort of miasma of unhappiness and managed to touch several of Dawn's men for small loans.

Whether they gave the money out of kindness, or as a sort of insurance against future sexual deprivation, she never knew, but Dawn thought very poorly of it. Lola, she said, was a bolting, bludging little bastard and Lola could go—cadging money from men she thought she was

86

too good to sleep with, money that could have better been spent on Dawn. Lola could go. So, Lola, who was almost demented with the pain in her lungs, went out and, as a last resort, rang her mother. But it was Saturday afternoon, her mother's afternoon off—not a propitious time at all to ring Mrs. Lovell.

A foreign voice answered the phone and said:

'Mrs. Lovell is in bed. Will I waken her?'

'Oh hell,' thought Lola. 'Yes, please, it's important,' she said.

The owner of the voice went away and Lola waited, fighting off the spells of cold dizziness that made the walls of the 'phone-box revolve around her. Then the voice was back.

'Mrs. Lovell seems to be sleeping very heavily. Will I try again, or is it better I take a message and give it to her in the morning?'

Lola had a vision of her mother, paralysed with brandy, lying on her back snoring with the false teeth half out of her mouth, but she was desperate, she decided to try again.

'This is her daughter speaking,' and she spoke clearly and slowly to prevent herself from bursting into tears. 'It is very important. I am in trouble. My mother is probably drunk, very drunk, but please try again, just once.'

'Well,' the middle-European voice was beginning to sound a little aggrieved, 'already I try twice.'

'Listen, I know I have a damn cheek to ask a Hungarian Countess to do anything, but if you would be so very, very good I would like you to make one more attempt to get my mother awake; or if there is an old Australian around

87

perhaps he would feel honoured to run upstairs for you.'
Here Lola burst into tears which must have had a softening
effect on the Hungarian noblewoman, Polish landowner's
wife, Czech doctor or Rumanian ex-millionairess on the
other end of the line, for this time she managed to get
Mrs. Lovell awake.

Lola was apprised of this when a voice, much slurred
but with an overtone of hauteur (damn cheek ringing at
this hour) came on to the line and said: 'Yes,' just that,
a peremptory 'yes', and then silence.

Lola knew that her mother was gazing bozz-eyed at
the 'phone and wondering how the hell she got there, so
she said:

'Mum, this is Lola here.'

'Who's speaking, who's there, what—' Mrs. Lovell's
voice trailed off into a series of jugglings with her teeth and
Lola, in despair, shouted:

'Oh please, sober up.'

'Sober up! What's wrong with you? I'll hang up, yes'
(Mrs. Lovell's voice was filled with satisfaction at the
prospect of thus punishing insolence). 'I'll hang up.' And
hang up she did, leaving Lola to drag herself back to
Dawn's room to pack her clothes and get out somewhere.
But every time she moved the pain in her side caught
her so sharply that she had to sit down to get back her
breath, and she spent most of the afternoon sitting in her
armchair gazing into space and feeling, in a dim unreal-
izing sort of way, that she was in such a hopeless hell of
misery and pain that she need not worry much about
anything.

'I must die soon at this rate,' she told herself, 'and then it will all be over.' She then remembered that it was her eighteenth birthday and she began to laugh, and Dawn came in soon afterwards and joined in the joke. Dawn was in a good temper again now. She had an American sailor (merchant service) on one arm and a bottle of cognac under the other, and the liquor she had consumed already that afternoon had pushed away, at least for a while, the fears that always crowded around the very roots of her heart—fears of being an old, fat, starving harlot. She felt full of well-being.

'Say, honey, you got a little friend my buddy can screw?'

She decided to mix business with pleasure.

'Let's take this poor kid to the party,' she said. 'Her man's away in the States and her mother's a drunk; she's just got out and she hasn't been too good. I've been looking after her. Come on, a party would do her the world of good on her birthday.'

'You eighteen?' asked the Yankee suspiciously. Privately he had thought she was about fifteen. 'My buddy don't want no jail bait.'

When he had been assured that she was not below the age of consent, and also that her illness was nothing to do with venereal disease, he said she could come to the party.

'I have to ask for my buddy,' he explained. 'He's kind of bashful.'

Lola had a cognac and said she felt much better. Then, while Dawn and Elwood were in bed, she had a long hot bath which eased the pains of pleurisy temporarily; but by the time they arrived at the party she could scarcely breathe.

It was a very noisy party. Half the crew of Elwood's ship had taken over a small sly grog that called itself a night club on Breakfast Creek Road. Dawn, who was now well away in her rôle of benefactress to starving delinquents, decided that what Lola needed was something hot to eat. So Lola found herself with a plate of spaghetti and meat sauce steaming in front of her, and the smell of oil and meat almost made her vomit. Somehow her head was hurting her so much that she had to struggle to distinguish one sound from another, and yet she decided that she could not be going deaf, because through the roaring in her ears she could hear Dawn's voice exhorting her in a kind of genial bullying:

'Get that into you, kid, go and get stuck into it.'

Lola laid down her fork and looked at the ring of faces round her and the oily food before her.

'I'm sorry,' she whispered. 'I can't.'

'Get it into you,' ordered Dawn, 'or I'll rub it in your hair.'

'Come on, baby, have another drink,' said Elwood. 'You're no good to any man the way you are.' Elwood's friend, who was quite a kindly kid when there was no audience around, looked at her anxiously, and then he was putting his hand around her breast and saying:

'You fretting about that guy of yours in the States? Forget about him, honey—he's spoiling our night.'

Then Lola struck his hand away and began to scream at them all:

'Leave me alone, all of you, can't you all see that I want to be left alone?'

Dawn sprang up and smacked her across the face.

'Shut up,' she said. 'Pull yourself together. Do you want the cops in?'

'Be quiet everyone,' said a Middle West accent somewhere at the end of the table. 'I got something to say to the poor kid. Now listen to me, baby. You listening? I got news for you.'

Lola leaned forward. He seemed to be sitting a long way away, but he did seem an understanding type and she tried to put what she hoped was a polite and interested smile on her face.

'You listening?' he asked again.

Lola nodded. She tried to concentrate, and then the face at the end of the table seemed to float towards her—a moment ago it had been almost unseen, now it was a distended horror of a face within about an inch of her own. Its eyes were wrinkled up into slots, the cheeks blown out wide—two monstrous bladders sucking in air and then the air was expelled in one long, loud, expert raspberry.

'Now, doll baby,' said the voice that apparently belonged to this nightmare face, 'don't go making any more rebop or I'll smack your pretty fanny for you.'

Everyone was laughing, so Lola laughed too. It would never do to let them know that she did not know what the joke was. And someone was saying, 'That's a good girl,' and pouring her a drink which she swallowed down, not because she wanted it, but because they all seemed to grow so angry with her if she were not obedient; and then everyone seemed to be dancing, and she was sitting all alone and she poured herself another drink. It was a long glass.

She went on pouring and pouring. No hope of filling that glass, and then she saw that it was filled. It was just a seven-ounce glass and she had poured liquor all over the table. She must go away. They would be furious. Dawn would start beating her again. That terrible face would come back. Luckily they would not find her because she was underneath the sea. The waves were roaring above her head, but she was not drowning, the waves were hiding her and she was sitting on a rock listening to the music coming from so far away. But she would make sure. She would just slip into the cave beneath the rock. But perhaps that was a mistake, for in the cave it grew very dark, and she had always been afraid of the dark, and a tiger came in and lay down beside her and the pain in her side grew so terrible that she did not know what was happening until she saw that the tiger, of course, was tearing her ribs away; but she must be quiet, she must not scream, she must stay with the tiger till Brownie came to rescue her. The tiger was preferable to Dawn and the rest. She must not scream. Brownie would not be long now. She had written to him. She must not scream.

The police found her there at about one in the morning. She was quite alone. All the rest of the party had gone. She lay beneath the table, covered in cigarette butts and the spaghetti and sauce which the jester from the Middle West had tipped over her, to keep her warm, as he said.

'This looks like the one Auntie Westbury rang about tonight,' said one policeman to the other.

They had dragged her out from underneath the table and were trying to make her sit straight on a chair and give her name and address, if any. 'She said she wanted her brought in for parole-breaking before she turned eighteen next week.'

'I am eighteen tonight,' Lola was momentarily lucid with hatred, 'as the old smiling ghoul well knows. She rang up and shelved me tonight because she has been sweating on this very night, just waiting to see me in the hands of the cops instead of in the Children's Court. A tiger is eating me,' she added in the same reasonable manner.

'Do you think she's stacking on an act?' asked the younger cop. 'Or do you think she's sick, or in the D.T.'s?'

'All three,' said the other cop. 'We'll get the doctor to have a look at her when we get in.'

So it was that Lola came back to sanity a couple of days later and found that she felt cool again, the pain in her side was much better and she was lying in bed in prison hospital.

She got three months for vagrancy and, as she had spent more than a month of her sentence in hospital, she managed to get through the remainder without too much trouble, and Brownie was waiting for her when she got out.

He stood in the burning sunshine outside Central wearing his Sears Roebuck jeans and a beautiful American jacket and his arms full of parcels—American clothes that he had bought for Lola and two dozen red roses that were beginning to feel the heat. He had been waiting since about nine o'clock and now it was eleven and Lola had just arrived. She was bustled out of a car by two police-women and taken inside for a few minutes. Then she was out on the street again; they began walking slowly towards each other—slowly as though they were afraid to meet and touch—and then, when they were near enough for him to see the tears on her cheeks, she broke into a run and he put out his arms and folded her in amongst the crushed-up clothes and the ruined red roses.

'Oh, Brownie,' she kept sobbing, 'I knew you'd come. I knew you'd come as soon as ever you could, so I was waiting for you and I was being true all the time, honest to God I was. I swear to God. I know they always try and make vagrancy sound like prostitution. Please, Brownie, you got to believe me. I swear to God, Brownie. I swear to God—'

'Hush,' he rocked her gently because it hurt him to hear her.

'It's O.K., darling. I knew you'd wait for me as long as there was any chance at all that I'd ever get back. I know you are sick and you couldn't get a job. Oh, darling, darling.' He began to laugh at her gently. She was racked with sobbing now. She was quite frantic with relief.

'Easy, honey, easy.' He dragged a blue silk scarf out of one of the parcels (it had a palm tree at each end and it said: 'Welcome to Honolulu'!) and began to wipe her eyes and his own indiscriminately. 'I was talking to a copper on the 'phone. He told me how sick you were and, look, we've got everything. I've got us a little flat over in West End and I've got three months' relieving work on the rugs. Three months in the Port of Brisbane, and I won't even have to think of going away; and when that cuts out I'll put myself on to the river roster and I'll just be a home-port man. Come on, darling, stop crying.'

Lola looked up. Her eyes were happy even though her face was still wet, and she mopped at her cheeks with the blue silk scarf.

'Brownie,' she said, 'if we don't put a foot wrong they can't touch us now, and we're going to be such a square old couple they won't know us. I'm never going back in there while there's a breath in my body. When we get short of dough, I'll get work. They'll never have the satisfaction of vagging me again.'

Brownie laughed and whistled to a taxi that was cruising hopefully nearby.

'That's the spirit, small one. Now get in this cab and we'll go home, and I'll show you all your lovely States-side presents.'

Lola leaned on the window ledge and looked down into the darkening garden.

It might be haunted, she thought, with the instinctive intuition that every garden planted long ago is haunted. And this was one of the oldest gardens in Brisbane—old, overgrown and neglected: magnolia, mango and paw paw trees shading the roses that had survived the years without care and reverted to their original single-petalled state; bougainvillaea that swarmed about the house as though to push it into the earth, and everywhere springing clumps of pampas grass and bamboo, making small jungles where the frogs croaked and the snakes hid and the children played in fine weather, till their mothers came and ordered them home, scolding and threatening, and warning them against snake-bite, and looking with unfriendly eyes at Lola and Mavis and their men.

'Soon it will be dark,' said Lola, 'and the wind will drop and the frost will come in from the Downs, stretching out its hands like big frozen claws to grab me and chill the marrow in my bones.'

'You've got me to keep you warm,' said Brownie.

Lola turned and smiled at him. She did not say: 'Brownie, you can keep me warm just as long as life or fate or whatever it is, or whatever people call it, allows you. In one second all this could go—the garden, the house and the two of us together. In one second there could be nothing but the wind howling across the place where we were.'

Instead she said: 'We're right for tonight anyway, so that's all we need to worry about. Now I'm going to shut out the frost and stoke up the fire.'

She closed the window with a strange little ceremonial flourish, as though she were finishing a ritual. For in the Brisbane winter the west wind blows all day across the city, and while the wind blows the sun shines clear and warm, so that you have only to get in the lee of a sheltering wall to be warm again; but at night the wind drops, and then the cold comes creeping in from the hinterland to nip the city right to the edges of the river and the shores of Moreton Bay.

So every night Lola went about the house, with her black woollen stole pulled right around her, shutting the windows, lighting the lamps, putting wood on the fire and stirring the soup in the pot. It was in truth a ritual, an invoking of domestic magic, drawing a ring of enchantment around herself and Brownie. And outside—outside was the rest of the world and everybody in it.

Mavis and Lyle were at the pictures. They had gone to five o'clock session and taken Sharon Faylene with them. Sharon Faylene, eighteen months old, not walking, not talking and heavily bronchial, should not have been out on such an evening, but Mavis, who was expecting another child in three months' time, was taking in all the shows she could.

'God knows when I'll get out when I have two of them on the hip,' she would say. And she was attempting to saturate her system in the glorious freedom of the shops, streets, hamburger joints, theatres and milk bars, against the time when, little by little, the walls of the kitchen would close around her for ever.

She was also adding to her collection of records against the dreadful day.

'At least I'll have some music when I can't get out any more,' she would say as she arrived home with another second-hand long-player under her arms. Then she would add it to the neat pile beside the radiogram, which had the distinction of being the only hire purchase she and Lyle had ever completely paid off. They had bought it soon after they had married, and they were married three days after they stepped off the migrant ship in Sydney. They had met on the ship, and Mavis was pregnant by the time they reached Australia; so they had married and set out for the lush tropical Queensland that Lyle had read about. Expecting something like a Pacific island—coconuts, blue lagoons and the works—they had, naturally enough, been disappointed in Brisbane. But not in each other—they were in love with the fierce absorption of people who supplied each other with the only emotional reality they had ever known. Mavis was an only child. She could scarcely remember her father who had been killed in one of the first air-raids on London. Her mother had sent her to the country, where she was presumed to be safer and was certainly not as damnably in the way as she would have been at home getting under foot and lousing up her mother's widowhood. Mother had gone into munitions and had almost married several Americans. When Mavis came home to London she was twelve—lumpy, uninteresting and adolescent. Her mother took one look at her and packed her off to a cheap boarding-school. In the holidays she sent her to the pictures. It seemed the only thing to do with her.

When she left school she went to live in a hostel, and when one of her fellow inmates decided to go to Australia Mavis decided to go with her. Her mother agreed.

'You'll be O.K. with Edie,' she said. 'It's a good idea.'

Actually her mother thought it a heaven-sent idea. She was not a bad woman. She was a good factory hand and fairly satisfactory in bed, and it had never occurred to her that she might have any other duties to perform in all her life. She just did not know what to do with a daughter, and Mavis was beginning to age her considerably. Australia was a very good idea.

Lyle was different. His mother was passionately interested in him and in all her six children. All born into the horror that was Newcastle in the thirties, they were fed and clothed and driven and educated and brought up somehow, amidst poverty and bleakness and soap and water and haddock and hard work. Like his brothers, Lyle went out to earn as soon as he reached school-leaving age, and by the time he was twenty he had decided to go to Australia as an assisted migrant. His mother was a woman of granite, but he owed her a great deal. She herself, at eighteen, had come south from the Highlands on her way to see the world. Marriage had trapped her in Newcastle, but to her youngest son she had bequeathed the spirit that sent the Scots and the Irish to the ends of the earth in the days when the ends of the earth were still places of wonder and mystery.

Lyle sailed, his heart singing and his head ringing with the glorious adventuring music. And as the ship pulled away from the dock, he saw on deck a big blonde girl leaning against the deck railing crying bitterly. She was crying as a child weeps—noisily and unbeautifully, blubbering and shaking, her hands up to her face; and sheer happiness had made him so kind that he went up to this girl he did not know and took her hands down from her face and smiled at her.

'Don't cry,' he said. 'There's fine times ahead where we're going.' She stopped sobbing and looked at him, and he saw that her mouth was soft and unformed and he wanted to kiss it and stop the bottom lip trembling. They stayed together all the afternoon, and that night he went to the cabin she shared with Edie. Edie, being no square, stayed up on deck, and Lyle gave Mavis the baby that almost killed her later in Australia.

Australia can be a very lonely country. Australians do not like migrants. There is no particular reason why they should. And Queenslanders go one step further—they don't like other Australians. Most particularly they hate those smarties from Melbourne and Sydney. Then, of course, Northern Queenslanders despise Brisbanites, and so on up to sturdy old chauvinists at the top of Cape York, who, upon occasion, show their contempt for members of more southerly tribes by eating them. This is considered to be going too far—actually it is just fine old Queensland hospitality carried to its logical conclusion.

So Brisbane was not like the tropical islands Mavis had seen on the movies; nor was it the roaring frontier town for which Lyle had hoped. There was no pioneering to do, there were no wonders to see—just the housing shortage; and neighbours who ignored them, and poor pregnant Mavis. No stimulation except the stimulation of disapproval—the locals looking with intolerant amusement at his pegged trousers and duck-tail haircut. Well, at least that was something. He went out and bought a black shirt and a motor bike. The bike was on time payment.

Brownie and Lola had known the radiogram before they knew Lyle and Mavis. It had been about twelve months ago when they were living in West End in a very small flat and Mavis and Lyle were on the other side of the street in a bed and breakfast robbers' cave, and day and night the strains of *Rock around the Clock*, *St. Louis Blues*, *My Baby rocks me with a Steady Roll*, *My Boy Flat-Top*, etc., interspersed with an occasional bagpipe record came floating across the road. Then, one morning as she was going to work, Lola saw Lyle tear past on his bike, and she told Brownie that evening that at least one other man in Brisbane was a sharp dresser.

'I pity him then,' said Brownie, who was feeling rather bitter, having been chatted by the police for twenty minutes only that morning for no other reason, apparently, than that he was wearing the pegged trousers he had bought in

Galveston. After that it was only a matter of time before Lola ran into Mavis in Nick Petrides' corner shop. Mavis had Sharon Faylene, clad only in a damp napkin, on her hip, and both were enjoying a raspberry spider. They both looked hot and sticky and Mavis said she would never have believed that anywhere could be so hot.

'You've got a lot to learn,' said Nick. 'Wait till it really gets hot. Wait till Christmas time.'

'Gawd,' said Mavis with feeling. 'Don't I know. Last year was my first here and I thought I'd die.'

Lola smiled at her. She was privately thinking that poor Sharon Faylene was the most horrifying child she had ever seen. She sat upon her mother's hip, red-eyed, white-faced, flabby and unsmiling, with a big heavy head she could not hold up straight and a dummy from which she refused to be parted. When she partook of her share of the raspberry spider her mother moved the dummy to one corner of her mouth and placed the straw in the other, then Sharon Faylene made horrid gurglings and a dreadful double suction noise that made the sensitive stomach roll.

'What a lovely kid,' said Lola guiltily. 'How old is she?'

'About ten months.'

'Is she sitting up by herself yet?'

Mavis looked perplexed. Later Lola was to notice that Mavis often looked perplexed when she looked at Sharon Faylene.

'They're not supposed to sit up till they start getting teeth are they?' she asked.

She did not sound very anxious. She just did not sound very interested; but Lola was too kind to say that Sharon

101

Faylene should have quite a few teeth if it came to that. She just dropped the subject.

She was longing to ask if Sharon Faylene were on to vegetables, but, in the circumstances, she thought it would probably be tactless.

Mavis surveyed the shelves.

'Dunno what to have for my lunch,' she said plaintively. 'You can't cook anything up there. We're not allowed use of the kitchen in the middle of the day, and in the evening you can't get near the stove, it's got so many people round it. I'll have a small tin of baked beans, I think.'

'How will you heat your beans?' asked Lola, who in her wanderings had developed a morbid curiosity regarding the horrors of dwelling in rooms, hotels, flats, boarding-houses, hostels, reformatories and so on. It was always interesting to compare notes. Some bedroom cooks favoured the up-tilted radiators, others the secret spirit stove, but Mavis was a true primitive.

'Oh I stand the tin in hot water in the bath,' she explained. 'I heat her bottle the same way.'

'Poor bitch,' thought Lola, with complete sympathy and understanding. Aloud she said, 'Have you tried getting a flat?'

'Have I ever?' said Mavis. 'But what's the use? It's hopeless when you have kids.'

She ordered up another tin of beans, three eggs and some Benger's food for Sharon Faylene, ticked them up and wandered out disconsolately—child under one arm, groceries under the other.

That was how they became friends. Brownie was glad. He had just shipped aboard the *Kimberley* to go to

Fremantle. He would be away a few months and he was happy Lola would not be entirely on her own.

'They'll be company for you,' he said.

So they were, for a couple of months, and then Mavis and Lyle set out for Sydney. In other words, they fled from Brisbane leaving their debts behind them. It was fun while it lasted. Lyle was happier than he had been in months. At dead of night he brought the precious radiogram across to Lola's flat: 'It's only a matter of time before we get everything settled up,' he explained grandly, 'and then we'll come back and collect it. If we leave it behind that old bitch over there will take it for back rent.' Indeed their landlady had been threatening this course of action for some weeks past, and the hire-purchase company had been threatening to claim the bike, and they owed Nick about eight pounds for groceries. As Lyle said, 'When you gotta go, you gotta go.' He was very fond of this phrase and repeated it frequently.

He had thought of Mount Isa, where money was good and jobs were plentiful, but every time he mentioned it Mavis said the heat would kill her and Sharon Faylene; and when he spoke of going alone she would collapse on the bed, such a pitiful sobbing blonde heap as would have made anyone give way out of sheer pity and irritation mixed in about equal parts.

'For God's sake, Lyle, let's stay together whatever happens,' she would beg. So Lyle evolved this romantic plan of running away to Sydney.

Everyone was very gay the night before they left. Final plans were discussed at Lola's to avoid all risk of eavesdroppers. Even so, they spoke in dramatic whispers, interrupted with much half-hysterical laughing.

'Now remember,' Lyle kept saying to Mavis, 'you're supposed to be taking Sharon Faylene into the City Hall for her injections and leave those three napkins on the line to put them off the track.'

Next morning he went off on the bike, ostensibly to work. Actually he had been out of work for almost a fortnight—a fact which had tactfully been kept from their landlady. About a quarter of an hour later Lola went down the street. She was wearing high-heeled scuffs, a wide black skirt spread over the stiffest underskirt in Brisbane and she carried a small wicker case. She looked cheerful, innocent and jaunty—in a word, Lola in her usual attire for doing a little morning shopping. She bought some bananas and a packet of rusks, and, strangely enough, a squashy plastic animal of no known species which smelt of caramel; then she waited on tram stop No. 7 till Mavis appeared with Sharon Faylene in her arms.

'How is she?' asked Lola with an anxious glance at Sharon Faylene, who looked positively debauched this bright morning.

'Grizzling all night with her teeth,' said Mavis, 'and she's had three teething powders already since yesterday evening. I do hope they don't move her bowels on the bike, I'm sure.'

'Here's a tram, thank God,' said Lola.

'Everything's going fine so far.' Mavis sounded almost cheerful again so Lola forbore to say, 'We haven't made home base yet.' But she felt it, and she must have known something, for when they got off the tram just outside the Palace Hotel they were met by Lyle with the sweat standing on his forehead. He said:

'This corner's alive with frigging coppers. One's had his eyes on me for ten minutes; I thought you'd never come. Listen, I'm getting across the bridge. I'll meet you there.'

Lola looked at the policeman on point duty and at another by the walls of the hotel, who was manhandling a half-caste prostitute who used the beat outside the South Brisbane station. It was obvious that he was working himself up into a very ugly mood, with great gulps of the glorious drug of brutality, and that within a few more seconds he would become dangerous.

'Let's get going,' said Lola. 'You'd better take me on the pillion, it doesn't look as strange as loading on Mavis and the kid and they'll think you've been waiting for me.'

They rode across the bridge and a few minutes later Mavis came puffing up, complaining, of course, of the heat. 'Shall we go up to the City Hall,' she suggested desperately. 'We've got to go somewhere.'

'God no, not there,' said Lyle with justifiable irritation. 'It's a hive of coppers too, and all their pimps drink in the "Albert".'

Where were they to go? That was the question!

Lola had a sensation, not new to her, that perhaps they should not go anywhere. Perhaps they should just evaporate and save the atom bomb the embarrassment. At last they decided to go to Coronation Drive where it was usually fairly quiet, and Lyle went ahead and the women dragged along—Mavis miserable and Lola angry.

'If you ask me, all Brisbane's full of coppers and all of them bastards,' she said, expressing in one concise sentence the full theory of central government of the sunshine State.

'Well, if I can't get somewhere to sit down on Coronation Drive I'll throw myself into the river,' threatened Mavis.

The teething powders now took effect a little earlier than the time forecast, and Sharon Faylene had to be taken into the ladies room of a pub and washed and changed. Lola did it and found that she wanted to weep.

'There you are, Sharo girl, right as rain again,' she said. 'I'm surprised at you dropping your guts to a few coppers. I'll carry her a bit,' she told Mavis. 'You'll be holding her in your arms enough.' So the little procession went on, and at last caught up with Lyle waiting for them under a jacaranda tree.

Mavis sank gratefully down on the seat under the tree, and then the case was opened and there, packed ready to transfer to the haversack strapped to the seat of the bike, were most of Sharon Faylene's poor little clothes, and a bottle ready mixed, a spare skirt for Mavis, and Lyle's black shirt and pegged trousers.

Lola packed the haversack in silence.

'I've got some clean napkins in my bag,' said Mavis, eager to show that she still had a full grip on the situation.

'And, Lyle! I remembered to leave those nappies on the line.'

Then they all fell silent, and suddenly Lola began thrusting the bananas and the caramel-smelling animal at Mavis and saying:

106

'Well, here's a few things. Try and persevere with her, Mavis, when she has her banana. I know she slobbers all over the place, but she does love it so; and do you really think all those teething powders are good for her? I think you ought to try a Dover tablet crushed up in orange juice. The orange juice will do her good if nothing else, and here's a fiver to come and go on, and you'd better get going now.'

Mavis leaned across and kissed her.

'You're a good friend,' she said, 'the only one I ever had in Australia.'

'Thanks for everything,' said Lyle, 'and goodbye for now.'

'So long.'

Lola watched the bike till it was out of sight, then turned and started walking back towards the city. It was not yet midday. She had all the time in the world. She was alone again. She felt the familiar feeling of loss and emptiness. She wondered if she would get herself a job, or if she would go to a show, or if she would go into the Grand Central and have a drink and see who was there, or if she would have some lunch in town and do some shopping; and she decided against all these things. She went home and locked herself up in the flat. She pulled down all the blinds and locked all the windows. Then she buried the clock under a pile of cushions so that she could not hear it tick; she turned the tap tightly, for she knew by past experience how a dripping tap could thunder through a muffled flat, and she went into her bedroom, stripped off all her clothes and crawled into bed. She pulled the sheet up over her head and straight away the sleep came swirling round her. She felt she was floating. She felt the soft warmth creep around her body and relax all her limbs, and so she slept away the whole afternoon—all the unendurable time. For she could take no more sudden partings—now they affected her like a sickness, a shock. Too often she had been brave and kept herself busy, gone to a show—now there was only sleep, and when she awoke she was reborn. It was about four o'clock that the noise from the street came filtering through into her wombworld, and she opened her eyes and lay on her back staring at the ceiling and stretching her arms above her head. Then, suddenly, she remembered that Mrs. Abbott (Mavis and Lyle's landlady) would very probably be over to enquire about Mavis and Lyle—their whereabouts, and, what was more to the point, the whereabouts of their few possessions—and she shot out of bed, tingling with excitement, ready for anything.

She wrestled and shoved the radiogram into the wardrobe and locked it there.

'Be quiet and don't growl if the old lady visits me,' she told it.

That important business over, she took time off to get into brassiere, briefs and matador suit. Then she brewed herself a cup of tea and turned the wireless on full blast. She danced around the kitchen, doing intricate little jive steps as she prepared the evening meal—poached eggs, baked beans and some spinach.

'Got to keep up the old strength,' she told the wireless announcer. She had eaten, cleared away the dishes and was sitting catching up on her mending when Mrs. Abbott arrived.

'I suppose you know what I've come about?' said that lady.

Lola said, 'Should I?' Then she turned down the wireless, and waited with the attitude of politeness and insolence, carefully blended, that she kept especially for landladies and women police.

'Do you mean to say that Mavis and Lyle never told you they were going?' said Mrs. Abbott.

Lola shrugged her shoulders.

'I know nothing about it,' she said. 'How do you know they've gone?'

"Course they've gone,' said Mrs. Abbott. 'Owing me a lot of rent, too. Did they say anything to you about selling the radiogram they used to have going night and day?'

'Mrs. Abbott, don't start talking to me as though you were a plain-clothes cop,' said Lola, 'or I'm liable to do the lolly.'

'I would have been entitled to take it for back rent,' said Mrs. Abbott.

'Well spoken for a landlady!'

Lola returned to sewing the sequins around the neck of her black jumper—the interview was over.

A few days later Mrs. Abbott sought to revenge herself by sending the man who came to seize Lyle's bike across to the Hansen's flat.

'They might know something about it,' she said.

Lola routed him in short order. Indeed, she pursued him right down to the garden gate, shouting the age-old war-cry of the sailor's wife when dealing with duns.

'If my husband were home from sea he'd deal with you. Very cheeky when there is just a woman by herself in the house...'

There can be nothing in all this world as terrifying as a poor weak little woman whose man is away at sea.

That night she wrote to Brownie.

'Sharon's nappies are still hanging on the line over at Abbotts. I see them every time I go past and they make me feel a bit low—they look so ragged and lonely, though I must admit they are becoming a beautiful colour, much better than poor old Mavis ever got them. The sun is bleaching them snowy. I wish old Abbott would take them down. They remind me of old Sharo, who wasn't such a bad little kid once you got used to the look of her—and the smell. Anyway, we mustn't be morbid. I suppose we'll see them all again some day, and meanwhile I am having victory after victory over the squares. Today a man came from the loan company...'

Here followed a ball to ball description of what Lola had said to the man and what the man had said to Lola.

But final victory was with the squares, for the police caught up with Lyle in Tweed Heads, and he was arrested on the double count of fraudulent debt and taking a motor-bike, the property of Universal Credit Loan Company, inter-State, and attempting to avoid repossession of the said bike. The Magistrate said that, but for the fact that the defendant had never been in trouble before and had a wife who was expecting her second child, he would have taken a much more severe attitude...

The defendant seemed to be on the fringe of the bodgie cult which doubtless had contributed to his foolish behaviour...In paroling the defendant he was giving the defendant a chance...

Lola, reading the *Courier Mail*, suddenly felt a strong rush of affection for Lyle, standing in the dock, wearing his black shirt and bodgie pants (doubtless now very shiny at the seat and knees), and for poor Mavis (doubtless now very pregnant and floppy), weeping in the court, and for Sharon Faylene, looking as though she had been grown under bags (and doubtless still sucking that trusty dummy).

Shortly after this Lola received a letter one morning which read:

Dear Lola and Brownie,

Doubtless you have read of us in the paper—in the social news—as Lola used to say. It was terrible while Lyle was in remand, but we are doing all right now. We are in that big, old, falling-down place at the end of Eastman Street, No. 20. Come down as soon as you can. I have ever so much to tell and cannot come up in case old Abbott sees me and wants to get some rent out of me. Please come soon. Longing to see you both and have a good laugh over old times. *Signed* Mavis.

P.S. Would you like to move in with us and take out the fiver we owe you in rent? Just a suggestion. If you would rather the fiver I can let you have it the pay after next.

Lola took the letter into the bedroom to Brownie. He had arrived home two days before and had paid off laden with wages, overtime and accumulated pay. Lola pointed to the postscript.

'What do you think?' she asked.

They pretended to discuss it sensibly, but both of them knew that unless No. 20 Eastman Street was a hopeless hovel they would go there. Lola summed it up:

'All that cheap rent, Brownie. We wouldn't have to work for ages. We could just be together.'

The two rooms Mavis and Lyle had taken over were terrible. The mark of Mavis's housekeeping was upon them. Terrible is too mild a word. They were hellish. In one corner stood a bucket of Sharon Faylene's napkins. They were soaking till Mavis got around to washing them. They looked as though they had been waiting some time, and in the meantime they were a prime attraction for the blowflies that zoomed around in heavy black swarms. In the other corner was a sink where cockroaches had frisked undisturbed for twenty-five years, and they were damned indignant about the intrusion of Mavis and Lyle. Against one wall was a doddering table, and on what had once been a gas stove there stood a two-burner primus. It was glued to the stove by a mixture of splashed fat and boiled-over stew; and when Lola and Brownie entered it was smoking away like a very old tramp steamer. It was heating a bottle for Sharon Faylene. Mavis had the bottle standing in a saucepan in which she was also boiling Lyle's white socks. Sharon Faylene, clad in the usual napkin, was crawling amongst the matches and cigarette butts that littered the floor. Occasionally she found a dead cockroach and Lola noticed her thoughtfully eating one, but decided it would be beside the point to mention it. And over everything poured the exhausting sunshine of a Brisbane March. It streamed through the window that could not be shut or shuttered. It streamed over the dirt and decrepitude and pointed up every hole in the floor and crack in the walls; and it turned poor exhausted Mavis into a perspiring heap, distressful to see, as she sat on a kerosene box pulling herself together with a cigarette. She shrieked, and then wept with delight when she saw Lola and Brownie.

'Gawd, it's good to see you again,' she kept saying, as she led them in to show them the bedroom. This was slightly better. True there was no bed. All three of them slept on a double-bed mattress and a pile of grey blankets thrown in one corner; and from the way they smelled it was obvious that Sharon Faylene had not yet been trained out of bed-wetting. But at least it was cool and quiet, and the door and window worked; and when Lola looked up she saw that the ceiling was high and beautiful, plastered in a design of scrolls and frond-like leaves, with here and there in the corner a hint of the gilding that the damp and weather had not yet washed away.

''Course it's a bit rough yet,' said Mavis. 'But when I get organized we're going to do wonders. Lyle's buying a bed this pay. He's got a fabulous job now in the Cold Storage. Gawd, I should be put into it myself.' She wiped her sopping brow and went on:

'The sink is not too good. Sometimes the water runs and sometimes it doesn't; and then, when you pull out the plug, there must be something wrong with the pipe because it just runs straight underneath the house, but

I don't suppose it matters because we're up on such high stilts anyway.'

'How is the dunny?' asked Lola, who had never quite become accustomed to the lack of sewerage and the prevalence of gastro-enteritis in Brisbane. 'Does it have a chain?'

'It does,' said Mavis with a touch of the house-proud in her voice. 'It's down under the house, and the wooden part of the seat has gone long ago, but there's plenty of water, plenty of it. In fact there's so much that the cistern flows over; and if you're going to be there any length of time you have to go down in your raincoat, and you should see all the ferns that are growing around it—terrific. Lyle calls it El Grotto. "Why bother to go to Capri?" he says.'

Brownie stood fingering a frond of bougainvillaea that had grown through a window and was creeping along the wall.

'Couple of seasons and this'll have all this wall down,' he said.

He took the heavy purple flowers, pushed them back outside and wrenched the shutter closed. The room was filled suddenly with gloom and dusk, and outside on the wooden shutters the bougainvillaea rustled angrily.

'Listen to it,' said Lola. 'It's furious, Brownie. This was one house it was going to eliminate and you've stopped it for a little while.'

Brownie was back in the kitchen looking at the wood stove.

'Does that work?' he asked.

'Don't know,' said Mavis. 'I've never tried it. Haven't been game.'

114

He rattled the flue and half a hundredweight of soot crashed down from somewhere.

'It should be all right with a bit of a clean out.'

He looked around, the fierce light of Scandinavian house cleaning in his eye.

'It would,' he said, 'take a bosun and six A.B.'s of the Wilhelmsen Line working bell to bell for six weeks to get this place clean. Still, it can be done. We'll stay.'

It was the day they moved in—a Saturday afternoon, still and sunny with the scent of the oleanders heavy on the air. Mavis, Lyle and Sharon Faylene had all gone down to the park to watch soccer practice. The house was silent save for the swish of Lola's skirts as she danced from room to room and her voice raised in an excited sing-song.

'Oh, Brownie, it's a beautiful old house.'

They had come in through the front door and there, right in the hallway, the magic started. Coloured light lying on the floor and the walls; coloured light from the red, blue and golden glass set around and above the door. Light lying like gilt around the black hair pulled high on the crown of Lola's head. Light the colour of old rose bathing the wondering face of the boy and girl as they stood there hand in hand.

Light like flame lying across the broken feet of a plaster Venus who stood, suitably draped, in a niche where she upheld a broken gas bracket. And down where the light fell away into darkness they pushed open another door with two broken panels and a handle of amber cut-glass and they were in what must have once been a dining-room. It was

115

wide and high: all its windows looked south-east, which is the only way to look in Brisbane, and all these windows were crammed with the purple arms of bougainvillaea so the glare from outside came through muted and beautiful. At one end was a fireplace such as has not been built in a Brisbane house since the turn of the century at least. It was like a small cavern edged round with Spanish tiles all glazed in a strange design of red and white roses. They were set alternately, first a white rose, then a red, and sometimes a jagged space, the work of time or vandals. It was all surmounted by an overmantel of cedar that had once been polished and carved into a design of vines and more roses that rioted over the myriad small shelves that had held the gilt clock, the Dresden Shepherdess, the Wedgwood jars.

'My head is getting dizzy with fancy fireplaces,' said Brownie as they walked into the second of the big reception rooms that lay one each side of the hall. 'Don't you think they're a bit much, dear? I mean, if simplicity is good taste and all that jazz.'

'I suppose they are,' Lola agreed; 'but I'm sick of simple little modern rooms big enough to hold a bed, a dressing-table, a wardrobe and a douche-can; all this mid-Victorian trimming cheers me up. I suppose I should find it all sad and ruined, but I don't. It just looks as though it has decorated a lot of living in its time, and it's ready to decorate a lot more if it gets a chance. Look at that,' she waved towards the looking-glass that rose above the mantelpiece, flanked by what were supposed to be small Grecian columns made of marble.

'Isn't it terrific? It reflects nearly all the room.'

Brownie went nearer and surveyed one of the columns closely.

'Someone has written "Harry and me camped here the night of August 14th, 1950,"' he said. 'Like you said, darling, it's seen a lot of living.'

Lola laughed and said, 'I won't be squashed. I'm in a poetic mood.'

They went out on to the verandah that ran round three sides of the house.

'I didn't know there was so much wrought iron outside New Orleans,' said Brownie.

It edged in the verandah to waist height. Like town lace, it ravelled round the house and the bougainvillaea and climbing roses twined amongst it.

On both the north and south sides of the house there were three bedrooms that connected with the verandah by french windows long since denuded of glass, and at the back of the house a narrow stairway of sandstone steps led down to the garden and the underneath of the house—to the wash troughs choked with weeds and the toilet surrounded by ferns and a bathroom that must have been a housemaids' hell of mirrors to polish, marble to clean, copper to burnish, a bath the size of a modest swimming pool; and no water laid on at all.

'They must have toiled up and down the stairs with buckets of water,' said Lola. 'Ah well, as I remarked to the Duchess only the other morning, I think the working-class was happier in those days.'

She sat down on the bottom step, and plucked a dog rose and held it crushed up against her cheek.

'Oh, Brownie,' she said, 'I can't believe it. It's all so beautiful. Let's stay here till our money runs out.'

When Mavis and Lyle and Sharon Faylene came home from the soccer the house-cleaning was already on. Brownie had picked the lock on the shed at the bottom of the garden and discovered two chairs, a chest of drawers and the most beautiful iron bedstead. Lola had been down the street and returned with hamburgers, cokes, sand-soap, bar soap, kerosene, phenol and Brasso. Brownie was scrubbing the bed, piece by piece, in his own special solution of kero, phenol and sand-soap, and as he finished Lola carefully polished the brass spikes, globes, crescents and assorted squiggles with which it was decorated.

'I do hope the landlord doesn't mind. He never said anything about furniture,' said English Mavis.

'Need the landlord know?' said Australian Brownie. 'Anyway, I'm not sleeping on the floor when there's a bed around for all the landlords in the world.'

So that night, when the possums peered through the holes in the ceilings of what had once been the blue bedroom they beheld a strange sight—an iron bedstead, freshly polished, was pushed against one wall and a stack of suit-cases stood in the corner. Across the wires of the bed were thrown an assortment of sheets and coverings, most of them bearing such markings as Union Steam Ship, Howard Smith, Brisbane Harbour Trust, and amongst this stolen linen, thrown together in the cleft where their weight made the bed sag almost to the floor, lay a human boy and girl. The possums crept forward in the moonlight and stared at the sleeping figures. The boy lay on his back, stark naked, his head thrown back, one arm folded across his chest, the other flung out in a protective curve around the girl. The girl looked very small beside the boy. Her long hair spread dark across the pillow and curled like a fetter across the strength of the boy's forearm. She wore a petticoat of torn black lace and one of the boy's shirts; but her face they could not see, for she slept with her hands shielding her head as a child lies in the womb. The little animals backed away. On the floor and the walls and even the ceiling they smelled the strange human smell of disinfectant and scrubbing, and for this, with sure instinct, they blamed the boy. But through the acrid, nose-itching aura of soap they smelled something else—something they knew—the infinitely older, erotic, heavy sweetness of the frangipani. Someone had gathered an armful and set it in a broken saucepan on the floor at the foot of the bed. This, decided the possums, was the work of the girl.

In the weeks that followed Brownie worked on that house as only a Nord can work. He scrubbed floors, mended shutters, cleaned the stove, threw out the gas stove, made shelves and tightened the wires of the bed.

And now began what was for all four the happiest time of their lives. Lyle did well at his job and Brownie got work on the harbour pilot boat, which meant he was usually home every night. Lola left work to have more time with Brownie and to help with the cleaning up and renovating. Within the first week Brownie had lugged home a second-hand interior-sprung mattress, and Lola had made a mosquito net for the bed out of pieces of netting she had picked up cheap at a job-lot shop. She used to sit on the top of the front steps, clad in her matador pants and skin-tight sweater, Brownie's battery set wireless beside her, and sew the net that frothed around her, while Brownie worked on repairs to the roof and Mavis sat smoking and staring into space, and Lyle nailed canvas across the french windows of the bedrooms. All this cheerful, if bizarre, domesticity, and so much hit-parade and pegged pants and young masculinity stripped to the waist and getting the sun stirred the locals to a frenzy of indignation. They spoke of the bodgies down in number twenty as though they were a collection of dangerous and habitual criminals. Lola, said the women, was no good. You could see at a glance she was no good. She reminded them, they said, of someone who had been in trouble, and they dug back in the recesses of their minds (ill-ventilated and sunless rooms, the walls papered with pages out of *Truth*, according to Brownie) and assured themselves that they were certain that they had seen Lola's picture somewhere.

'It was when the cops raided that place in Margaret Street,' they said.

And now she was living with that young sailor. It was a shame. He calls her his wife. They would never believe that, but she was just the sort who would always get a man to keep her. Not that she'd have any children. That sort never did. Much too sly. Not that it was to her credit. Quite the reverse. There was that other poor big slob. She was expecting again. It shouldn't be allowed. She had no idea how to look after the one she already had, and it wasn't walking yet. Some husbands had no decency. It seemed it was very difficult to satisfy the good ladies of West End as to suitability for parenthood—some were too crafty, some too silly, and in the meantime Lola, Brownie, Mavis and Lyle went on their way uncaring. They were living by their own rules and happy in the process—a sight to arouse anger, hatred and resentment in any suburban street. And while they sewed and cooked, scrubbed, made love and danced to the music of the battery set the old house won back a little of its bloom and was no longer derelict. It was a real human shelter again with even a baby between its walls, and Sharon Faylene began to bloom. She began to pull herself up by the furniture and try to walk around; and she began to say a few words that could be translated, with a lot of love, as 'Hi' and 'Dadda' and 'Auntie Lole'. All this was mostly due to Lola, who had a genuine, if disorderly instinct for housekeeping and children, and who had, during both her pregnancies, done a little reading on the subject. It was she who decided that Sharon Faylene should be on mashed vegetables—should have been on them long ago—and Sharon Faylene, who apparently had been sick and tired of over-sweetened milk and fancy biscuits, took to more savoury foods with a will. She had her vegetables with a little salt and plenty of butter, and broth with Oxo cubes added for extra strength, and occasionally a small piece of chicken, and a bit of T-bone steak to chew every Thursday night.

'Got to get the old strength up for Friday,' Lola would say.

'I never saw a child come on like our bubby has,' Mavis would say. 'She'd do anything for you. Say "Hi, Auntie Lola".'

Sharon Faylene surveyed her mother, owl-eyed, then she burped and went on chewing her underdone steak. Her teeth were coming late, but she was proud of them and enjoyed playing cannibals on T-bone night.

As May wore on and the first winds thrust in through the chinks in their shelter Mavis tried pasting pictures of film stars over the cracks in the walls. Assisted by Lola and Sharon Faylene, she had a plentiful supply. The baby girl sat on the floor handing up pictures of the famous registering delight, wistfulness, tragedy or sexual frenzy, and remarking of all, irrespective of putative sex, 'Pretty lady, pretty lady.'

That night was chilly. The cold wakened Lola at about one o'clock and she crept, shivering and complaining, out of bed to look for a pair of Brownie's woollen deck socks, and to spread his duffle coat across the foot of the bed. Pulling on the socks and huddled in the duffle jacket she stood at the window for a while. The night was still and beautiful; not still with the languorous restfulness of a summer night, but held motionless in a cold stillness, so that the garden was like the enchanted garden in an old story; and the stars hung in the sky like polished steel, and the footsteps of someone passing in the night rang on the hardening ground. Then, as the girl looked into the moon-stricken garden she saw, first running along the top of the bamboos and then, a little stronger, bending the branches of the oleanders and frangipani, the first ripple of the west wind. Afraid, she crept back to bed, and Brownie stirred in his sleep and gathered her in against the warmth of his body.

'Where have you been?' he asked, half asleep.

Lola could not keep her fears to herself.

'Oh, Brownie,' she said. 'I saw the Westerlies arrive.'

'One thing's certain,' said Brownie; 'those bloody silly pictures will never keep it out. I'll get some putty tomorrow and do a proper job.' He hugged her against him. 'I'll make sure the wind doesn't blow cold on you.'

Lola laughed at him.

'You be the caveman, and sleep across the mouth of the cave to keep away the evil spirits and the sabre-toothed tigers,' she said.

Brownie thought this a pleasing plan. He fell asleep, unafraid of the tigers of this or any other age; but the woman who crouched behind his shoulders lay awake staring into the dark. In the morning they found the pictures of the famous, still registering delight, wistfulness and sexual frenzy, crumpled and torn, blown into the corners and under the furniture or hanging in strips from the walls— poor pretty ladies, poor pretty ladies.

So Brownie puttied up the cracks in good sea style, pressing in the putty with his thumb and smoothing it with a deck knife, and Mavis dipped again into her library and came forth with more glossy portraits to paste over the repairs.

'Look at old Sharo,' she said. 'Proper film fan she's getting. She knows Rita Hayworth from Lana Turner already. You know, I never thought I'd fall in once—let alone twice.'

Lola was up on a packing-case, paste-pot in hand, putting up the pictures as Mavis handed them to her. She asked:

123

'What made you think you'd never fall in?'

'Well I'd been lucky till I met Lyle. 'Course, I didn't like it much till I met Lyle if it comes to that. I only did it to oblige, as you might say. But Lyle is different.'

'You might have known a Geordie would get you up the spout as quick as look at you,' said Lola, who had the traditional respect for the virility of north-country men.

Mavis seemed unconvinced.

'Suppose so; but look, it never seems to happen in the pictures like that. If they make a picture about people having a baby, they make it real light-hearted, and they've got everything for the kid an' all; the mother-to-be is knitting; they're not worrying about money, and they have one of those real fabulous Hollywood homes. Anyway, who would think I'd be so stiff as to fall again? I used fizzers, too, because they told me to take care. It took me five days to have Sharon Faylene and then they had to cut her out. They said another one might kill me.'

Lola had long ago lost her capacity for healthy horror, so now she looked at her friend with the complete absence of hope that had taken its place.

'You mean to say,' she said, 'they told you another kid might kill you and yet they didn't tie your tubes or anything?'

'No. I asked one doctor what I should do, and he said "make your husband sleep on the roof".'

Lola forbore to say what she thought of such very ethical humour.

'In Sydney,' she said, 'they'll fix you up with a Dutch cap at a place called the Racial Hygiene Bureau, or something like that.'

124

'Nothing like that in Brisbane,' said Mavis.

'No,' Lola agreed with venom. 'Nothing like that in good old, sweet old, wholesome, pure little Brisbane, best little town this or any side of the Black Stump, where the old-fashioned virtues are practised, and familes are large as of yore, and the peasants are contented, if poor. God, how I detest this cruel bastard of a place!'

Mavis began to laugh.

'You're fabulous when you get sarcastic,' she said. 'Anyway, I suppose I could have got fixed up, but I didn't have any money, and I wasn't game to have a go at it myself.'

'Hell, no,' agreed Lola.

'Anyway, now it's too late.'

'Yes, I don't think anyone for any money in the world would touch you at five and a half months,' said Lola, whose knowledge of human greed was extensive, but not yet complete.

'No, nobody would touch me at five and a half months that's for sure,' said Mavis. 'Look at Sharon kissing Tony Curtis.'

'Don't you think you should go and have an examination or something?' Lola was anxious. 'People are supposed to be examined every month when they're pregnant.'

'Oh, I did when I was about two months. I went up and booked in as soon as I got back to Brisbane, and they said nothing about stopping it so I can't be in any danger after all. They stop a pregnancy if there's any danger to the mother's life, don't they?'

'Yes, that's right, so they do.' Lola knew that this was true of Sweden: she was doubtful if it applied to Queensland, but she decided it would be kinder to keep her doubts to herself.

She sat down on the top of her packing-case.

'Nevertheless, Mavis,' she said, 'I think you're lucky to have your baby.'

'Couldn't say,' said Mavis, 'what makes you think so?'

'Well, like I told you a long time ago, I've lost two. The first time it was my own fault. I let my mother get rid of it. Well, it's a terrible feeling. A real bad feeling.'

'Can't see it was your fault. You were only a baby yourself.'

'Maybe—but if I'd put on a real struggle there was nothing my mother could have done. I could have said I'd go to the police or something.'

'Hell! You can't copper on your own Mum.'

'No, of course not; but I could have just threatened or something. Oh, I could have done something.'

Lola began to cry, turning her head, hysterically, from side to side.

'You see,' she went on, 'I know what I'm talking about, because when I sat there in Dawn's with the pleurisy I was nearly a week there, feeling like I was going to die, and the only feeling I had left was sorrow about that baby. I'm going to die, I would think, and there'll be nothing of me left at all because I let them kill my life. I can't tell you, Mavis, how I wanted a child then—some of my own life to leave behind.'

By this time Mavis also had the tears streaming down her face.

'Lola love,' she begged, 'don't think about it. It never does any good to think about things.'

Lola produced a handkerchief and wiped her eyes.

'I shouldn't be upsetting you, that's for sure,' she said. 'We don't want to go upsetting your milk supply or something.'

Mavis shrugged her shoulders.

'I never seem to make milk. Last time I was dry as a bone. Poor old Sharo was on the bottle right from the beginning. Not that she was very hungry, though. She was a big baby, too, but she just seemed to want to sleep all the time. That's why I had such a bad time they said. She was too big.'

Lola leaned forward.

'Look, Mavis,' she said, 'I got a terrific book when I was in the Horror Chambers. I'll give them that. They got me this mighty book all about what to eat to keep your baby a nice convenient size and exercises to do to make your muscles strong. I used to do my exercises every morning.'

'Gawd!' Mavis looked down at her swollen girth. 'Can you see me doing kicks at this stage—Mavis the performing elephant!'

Lola laughed.

'But didn't they put you on a diet or anything?'

'Oh, they said something about oranges and steak and milk and that, but I never took much notice. Lyle was in remand then, and I was living on cokes and cigarettes.'

Lola nodded.

'Isn't it always so? The world's full of greedy bastards who are ready to charge you fifty quid for an abortion, or flinty-faced old squares who are just busting to see you have the toughest labour going; but there aren't many in between who want to teach you anything about it.'

Mavis laughed.

'It wouldn't do any good telling me,' she said. 'I couldn't keep all that jazz in my head anyway.'

'But it makes it interesting—it truly does.'

'Not for me it wouldn't.' Mavis was firm. 'As far as I'm concerned housekeeping and having kids is strictly for the old folks in Squaresville. Look how you hated being with old Westbury. You said yourself it was worse than jail, and she was wonderful at cooking and scrubbing and everything.'

'Yes, but she really hated it.'

'I don't hate it.' Mavis was trying to work things out. 'And I love my kid, of course; but I can't really take an interest. You know what I'd like to be doing now?'

'No?'

'I wish I was eighteen again, and slim and light on my feet; and I wish it was Saturday night and I was at a party, and I'd jive all night, and I'd be wearing my—' She broke off, and gestured helplessly. 'I don't know how it happened,' she said, 'but suddenly everything like that is over, everything is gone.'

'It'll come again. Never mind, Mavis; I'll baby-sit every now and then and you and Lyle can step out. You'll be the sharpest young couple in town.'

She looked with pity at the pregnant woman and the baby girl playing with the film magazines. Suddenly she put down the paste-pot and jumped down from the perch.

'You'll be all right, kiddo,' she said. 'We've done enough work for today. How about we leave the stew, it'll keep till tomorrow, and go down to Dan's and have a steak for tea? If we get down there early we'll get the juke box.

We can leave a note for the boys to come down and join us. Come on, I want to hear some music and see some people.'

Dan's was easily the toughest hamburger bar on South Side. The police turned it over on an average of once a night, and Brownie, Lola, Mavis and Lyle ate there about once a week. It was their version of dining out. They liked Dan's. They liked the smell of frying onions, sizzling meat and terrible coffee. They liked the colour scheme of blue and yellow, the juke box jumping out its rhythmic de-celebration, and they liked the company of their own kind.

When the girls arrived there were only three other customers present: a girl in a tight black dress and shoulder-length diamante earrings, her offsider—a plain poor child in a tight skirt and sweater and an unfortunate attempt at a short widgie haircut, and one adolescent boy who was drinking coke with them, and feeling very sharp to be spending his afternoon in the company of a woman whom the police had ordered out of town that very day. It was the girl in black who had achieved this social distinction. She had arrived from the country six months earlier and had drifted from waitressing to sporadic prostitution. Her knowledge of prophylaxis being but indifferent, she had become diseased, and in due course was picked up by the police. Her people being solid farmers in the Ipswich district, the police were easier with her than they would have been with a genuine waif—they merely ordered her home and put her on a bond. She was to keep out of Brisbane and report to the local Health Officer for treatment. She had been sitting in Dan's holding court all the afternoon, but now she looked at Lola and knew that her moment was over. Lola, in her spreading skirts and high-heeled scuffs, her breasts half naked, her eyes drowned in mascara and her hair caught back in a pony tail, was a scene-stealer in any bodgie's book. She came swishing into Dan's with Mavis and Sharo in tow, and they were also in gala attire. Mavis wore tight velvet slacks with pegged cuffs and a maternity smock made specially to cope with winter chills—scarlet corduroy, finished off at the neck with a huge bow. Mavis's English face looked very clear-skinned and pretty above that scarlet bow.

Sharo wore her pink brushed bunny wool and her bunny slippers. They were three formidable women, and Brownie, when he looked in twenty minutes later and saw them just about to attack their steak, burst out laughing.

'Man! There's a whole lot of female in this booth,' he said. 'Hello, honey, that sweater—one deep breath and your norks will be in my soup.'

'Seventeen, seventeen, cool and solid seventeen,' sang the juke box.

'Got any more sixpences?' said Lola as she kissed him. 'I'm in the mood for music.'

Sharon Faylene began waving a soup spoon and yelling, 'Daddio'—an improvement on 'Dadda' which she had achieved with much coaching—and there was Lyle coming through the door.

'This is grand, this is,' he said, as he bent and kissed his wife and daughter. 'A man comes home from work and finds the whole family parked around the juke box. What is happening to good old-fashioned family life. Did you order me a steak, doll baby?'

This last question was addressed to Sharon Faylene, and Mavis answered for her.

'The biggest in the place, darling, that's what you're getting.' And she reached over and patted his hand.

'I love you, you pregnant pest,' said Lyle. 'I love you all the time, and I'm going to make a fortune for you.'

The meal over, Mavis said she felt like a drink.

'She's maddened with steak and rock and roll,' said Lyle. 'Will you listen to her? Come on then, I'll buy you some Guinnesses. "A baby in every bottleful".'

He quoted this last in a sort of sing-song chant, and then explained to a startled lad at the next table:

'We've decided to make it triplets—one at a time gets lonely.'

Mavis was almost weeping with laughter.

'Who'd ever be bored with a madman like you around,' she said.

And then they were out on the street again, and making for the Wheatsheaf Hotel, which was just around the corner and had a beer-garden that was sheltered from the wind. It was one of those nights when exhilaration is in the very air, with a North wind that sometimes comes, charged with electricity and whisperings in the air, into Brisbane in winter: a memorable wind that always makes the heart beat a little faster, and the limbs tingle with an added energy, as though with some magic borne down out of the regions that have no winter at all.

And everything seems good. And so it was that night. The almost deserted beer-garden, quiet within its sheltering brick walls while the wind sang on overhead, blowing down towards the South to become a snow-laden demon by the time it arrived in Melbourne: the stars glittering with draught; the geraniums growing in shadowy corners, spicy red bunches around darkened stems; the laughter coming from the bar inside and the hotel cat that stood up on its hind legs and patted Sharon Faylene gently with its paw. And everything was something to laugh about. The way Sharon Faylene insisted on having a sip out of everyone's glass and finally fell asleep, very red in the face and snoring loudly on her mother's lap: and the way Mavis kept insisting that she had a craving for stout, and she must have everything she fancied; how she had to keep dashing off to the ladies.

'Two pints in a one-pint bladder, that's the trouble,' said Lyle, which struck them all as very witty indeed. And then Lola got to the stage where she laughed at everything—as sooner or later she always did. She took off her earrings because they were hurting, and while putting them on again she dropped one of them down the front of her jumper, and laughed so much she could not get it out, and Brownie had to fish for it.

Then Mavis said she was hungry again, and Lyle went out and bought salted peanuts and potato crisps, and Brownie, not to be outdone, bought another supply.

'Old soaks, that's what we are,' said Mavis happily. And she ate so much, washed down with more stout, that she seemed to swell visibly, and had to undo another button of the maternity slacks, which made them bag around her hips most alarmingly. And by now a change had come into the atmosphere. They laughed a little less, and Brownie

132

and Lyle drew closer to their women and began to handle them around.

'Let's go home,' said Lola. Brownie's thigh was pressed hard against hers, and his arm was around her shoulders. 'Let's not be the last to go. Thrown out at closing time with the sleeping child clutched in our drunken arms.'

'Yes, let's go now,' agreed Lyle, 'while the drink's still only in our heads.' And he led the way with Sharon Faylene over his shoulder and Mavis hanging on to his arm; and as he went he sang to a little tune of his own composing:

'Oh pregnant in the winter and barefoot in the summer, that's the way to keep them if you want to be the boss.'

Lola and Brownie brought up the rear, walking arm in arm, with their faces pressed close together.

'If I don't get you home soon,' said Brownie, 'I'm going to bust.'

So they went home. Brownie threw himself on the bed and pulled off his jumper and skivvy all in one movement.

He stretched out his hand.

'Come here.'

'Wait,' said Lola.

She moved around the room, the drink warm in her stomach and making her head and limbs feel light and dreamlike. She pulled off her black stole and pulled the black jumper over her head.

'Hurry up,' said Brownie.

But she moved slowly, naked to the waist now, unpinning the long black hair so that it fell around her shoulders, putting perfume on her nipples, swinging her skirts around, undoing them and letting them fall to her feet. Every movement deliberate, provocative, as she went about the business of contraception—turning her body from that of a living woman into a sterile doll. And when she was ready she tinned down the lamp and held out her arms to the half-maddened boy on the bed.

'Now love me,' she said. 'Love me every way you know how.'

Afterwards, when she lay exhausted, already drifting into sleep, her head against his shoulder, Brownie put out his hand and patted her hair.

'God, you're beautiful,' he said.

'You're beautiful too.'

'I wish I never had to go away. Why can't we be together every night like this?'

'We'd never last, Brownie. We'd wear ourselves out. No, darling; don't worry about other nights in the future. Maybe you won't have to go away. Maybe we'll win the lottery. And anyhow, whatever happens, this is one wonderful night we've had and it is already the past. It cannot be taken away from us. One more good time before the atom bomb blows us all up and no strings attached—no lagging, no vagging and no kids.'

Brownie still stroked her hair. He said:

'Yes, you're certainly a lot more careful. Once you didn't care if you got a kid or not.'

'Do you want a kid?'

'I've always left that up to you. I was just saying that you've changed a bit.'

'Yes, I've changed. I'm not really half such a nice person as I was. I suppose that sounds silly to say, Brownie; but it's true. I suppose I seem better now. I'm nineteen. It's fairly normal to have a man at that age. When you're a little girl of not quite fourteen, people just think you're a baby nympho. But it wasn't like that really, you know. I didn't really want to be made love to. Please don't be hurt, Brownie. I've always loved you. But I was too young and too small, and it hurt my body, and I wasn't ready for it all. I'm the type to marry young and so are you, and I would have been just as happy to wait till I was sixteen or seventeen; but I couldn't wait, you see, because I had to be loved, and you were the only person I could turn to for love. No one wanted me except you; and all I thought of was how to pay you back. You could have got me to do anything. And look where that got us.'

'In the end, honey, it got us right here together.'

'Only after a lot of trouble, Brownie. A lot of hell I wouldn't wish to live through again. No, you can say what you like, life's really pretty crummy, and if you go doing a generous action towards it, like having a baby, then you're leaving yourself wide open, and life takes the opportunity to kick you right in the face. No, I'm going to be mean from this on and just live for the kicks that are pleasant.'

Brownie laughed drowsily.

'What's brought all this on?' he asked—knowing full well that she would probably be saying the exact opposite at breakfast time. Suddenly the cruel knowledge that she had kept pushed to the back of her mind all evening came rushing back at her, and she could think of nothing else. She wanted to tell him: 'Mavis, poor old defenceless Mavis is going to die because she had a second baby: and even if

135

she lives will she be any better off? A child is just one more person to agonize over.' But she said nothing. It was not fair to infect others with your own fear and distress. At any rate, Brownie was asleep, and she put her head against his outspread hand and went to sleep too.

It was about midnight one night late in September that Lola was awakened by movement in the next room, and then a shaky giggle from Mavis. Lola sat bolt upright in bed and shook Brownie.

'This is it,' she said.

Brownie muttered something incoherent, but Lola was already out of bed and pulling on clothes. Going into the kitchen she found Mavis and Lyle.

'Here we go again,' said Mavis.

'Well, let's get going for God's sake,' said Lyle.

Mavis laughed.

'That pain's gone,' she said. 'The next one won't come for a while. There's plenty of time. I'm going to have some tea.'

Lola had already blown up the fire still in the stove and put on the kettle. Brownie came out and they drank tea together and made all the usual jokes that people use when they're frightened, but not too frightened; and every time Mavis flinched with pain Lyle besought her, 'Don't drop it here, Mave, whatever you do. I'd go off with the shock.'

He was the picture of a distraught young father as he sat on the traditional suit-case and steadied his teacup in both hands.

'I hate to leave,' said Mavis. 'We're having such a good time.'

Lola looked round the ring of light that the lamp drew around them all, and at the shadows waiting for them in every corner, and she said like a hostess:

'Don't go yet. Do have another cup of tea.' ('Don't go out into the dark, Mavis, don't go.')

'Don't mind if I do.' Mavis entered into the spirit of this macabre tea-party. 'I don't know when I've enjoyed a labour so much.'

'Let me get a taxi,' begged Lyle.

'I'll get the taxi,' said Brownie. 'You stay here, Lyle, and be a bit longer with Mavis.'

Mavis started on her third cup of tea.

'It all helps to grease the slip-way,' she said.

Then Brownie was back with the taxi, and Sharon Faylene was awake and being carried out to kiss her mother goodbye; and then Mavis was driving off, hunched over in sudden pain, but still waving gaily and calling:

'Come and see my son at visitors' time this afternoon.'

'We'll bring champagne,' they called, 'and we'll have a party!'

Lyle came back about an hour later. Lola was awake, sitting in the kitchen rocker with Sharon Faylene sleeping on her lap. The coffee pot was keeping warm on the back of the stove and Lyle helped himself.

'They told me not to ring before midday,' he said, 'so I might as well go to work and I'll ring up at lunch time.'

Lola rang also at lunch time and was told:

'Mrs. Blackmore's baby is not born yet.'

She rang twice again during the afternoon, but the baby had still not arrived when they all (Sharon Faylene included) went up to the hospital that evening.

An over-worked and irritable nurse stopped them and said to Lola:

'You can't take that baby in. Mrs. Blackmore is in very advanced labour. Her husband can see her for a few minutes, that's all. She'll be going into this ward soon.'

They were standing straight outside the door of the ward indicated, and from it came a constant babble of suffering, with here and there an individual cry rising above the rest.

An Italian voice kept repeating:

'Oh Maria, Oh Santa Maria, Oh Jesus Maria.'

And an Australian voice called upon some absent husband:

'Oh, Johnny, Johnny, what have you done to me!'

'When she goes in there,' said the nurse, 'no one can see her, so whichever one of you is her husband had better go across to 15C there. She's in the end bed on the left side. The rest of you wait out there, and don't bring the baby up again.'

They were not waiting long for Lyle. He came out within a quarter of an hour. He was very white, and there were red marks around his wrists. He rubbed them as he spoke.

'The water just broke: she's in real big pain now. She hung on to my wrists like she would break my arms. They're taking her into the ward where babies are born. It won't be long now.'

138

But it was a long time, and in the end they were sent home. Lyle had eaten nothing since lunch time and it was obvious that any attempt to feed him would only end in his choking, so Lola mixed him a whisky and hot milk, and when he had finished that she mixed him another.

In the early morning came Nina Petrides from the corner shop. Lyle had given the hospital the Petrides' 'phone number and now they wanted to speak to him. It was not quite five o'clock. Nina was in a red silk dressing-gown with her black hair streaming around her.

'Run, run for your life, Lyle,' she shrieked, 'and if you need money for a taxi, take it from the till.'

Lyle was already off. He scrambled into shoes and jeans and pulled on his jumper as he ran. He was back inside a couple of minutes.

'They wanted to know will they operate,' he said. 'They say it may kill the kid. What do I care about the kid?'

Lola and Nina instantly blessed themselves in opposite directions. Such a statement made them afraid. Nina went off to light a couple of extra lamps before the icon, and Lola took Sharon Faylene into bed with her.

'Now,' she thought, as she tucked the child in between herself and Brownie, 'now Mavis will be under the anaesthetic, and now is the worst time of all the day or night. It's not the night, not the day. I hate these hours from four o'clock till seven. Oh God, don't let her die, don't let her die.'

Lyle arrived at the hospital just in time to be told that his son was dead and his wife must have an immediate blood transfusion.

139

He gave the blood and came home and slept a little while, then he went back in the afternoon.

At about three o'clock he rang Nina and sent a message to Lola to bring Sharon Faylene to the hospital. Mavis wanted to see them both. Lola left a note on the table for Brownie, took Sharon Faylene with her milk in a bottle and a change of nappies, and set out. Mavis was unconscious when Lola arrived, but after a while she rallied a little and Lola took the child in to her.

'Mumma,' said Sharon Faylene, and Lola lowered her to kiss her mother's cheek. A nurse was present and raised her eyebrows above her sterile mask; but this was merely force of habit. She knew, and Lola knew, that an extra germ or two would not make much difference to Mavis now.

Sharon Faylene set to work happily practising her walking round and round the benches in the waiting-room, and Lyle and Lola sat down to wait. After tea Brownie arrived with a blanket for Sharon Faylene, which was as well, because Sharon Faylene, after a full, exciting and novel afternoon was disposed to have her milk, an apple and some sandwiches from the canteen and go to sleep—which she did, wrapped in the blanket and rocked in Lola's arms.

Visiting time came to an end. Other people went home, but they were allowed to stay. A nurse came and told them they could wait outside the ward, and they sat there huddled together, trying to help Mavis stave off death; but the night wore on, and nurses and doctors came and went, and towards midnight they called Lyle to go in alone.

Mavis was conscious, and she had been weeping. Now she was long past any such effort, but her face, against the

140

pallor of approaching death, was swollen and blotched and misted over with tears, and as he bent over he saw that her bottom lip was trembling. Gently he kissed it and it steadied, and as on that first day they met, he saw the fear leave her eyes. With some strength that only love could have called forth she managed the shadow of a smile, and his name formed on her lips. She had no strength to give it sound, and then it came with the last life in her body:

'Stay with me, darling. I'm O.K. with you.'

It was so distinct a whisper that for a moment he almost hoped.

'I'll stay right here, darling,' he answered. 'Now sleep.'

Then he knelt beside her and put an arm gently under her head. He held her so, and in a few minutes she died gently and painlessly and without fear.

Early in the morning he came back home to Brownie and Lola, and from then onwards, till they got poor Mavis into the earth three days later, he cried. He sat in the garden with the tears rolling out of his eyes, and he ate nothing and smoked a great deal. Lola, who never cried much over an established fact, got her grief over in one long, passionate outburst of weeping on the night of the death; after that she spent her time brewing coffee for Lyle, and getting Sharon Faylene's clothes ready for the social worker who was to call and take the little girl to the State Home on the second day after Mavis died. Lola washed napkins, pressed night-dresses and mended and cleaned generally. She worked in a kind of cold fury, stopping every few minutes to hug Sharon Faylene and assure her:

'At least, kiddo, you're going in smart.'

She took the child into Coles and bought her overalls with a rabbit on the bib and slippers with bells on the toes. Sharon Faylene derived tremendous joy from those slippers; they tinkled when she walked, and she kept trying to dance and draw more music from these wondrous things on her feet. She sat down, she pulled them off, she chewed them, she rattled them, and in the end she kissed them. It was her last night home, and she seemed to be having a very good time, but once she stopped and looked around and asked:

'Where Mummy?'

And she refused, absolutely, to go into her cot. She insisted on sleeping with Lyle. Lola heard him sobbing in the night, and went in to him and said:

'I'd take her you know, Lyle, but I wouldn't be allowed. I'm an old lag like yourself.'

'Sharon you mean?' asked Lyle.

'Of course, who else would I be offering to take.'

'I'm sorry, I was thinking about Mavis.'

Lyle began to cry again, and Lola got him some cigarettes, felt Sharon Faylene to see if she were still dry, and then went back to bed.

Lyle and Mavis had never quite realized that they had had Sharon Faylene. Perhaps now it was just as well. Then she heard Lyle call from the next room:

'Lola, will you give her to the Welfare woman tomorrow. I don't think I could do it. I don't think I can bear to be around.'

The Welfare woman came up the drive next day and was pleased with what she saw. There was washing on the line, there was no stack of bottles around. Someone had painted the front door; the roof was mended.

'Poor little things,' she told herself. 'Somebody has tried.'

And she resolved not to lose kindness, no matter how she was greeted.

She was greeted with a wave of silent hostility enough to knock even a social worker off her feet. She saw a girl sitting on the floor playing with the baby. The girl was dark, wearing tinsel-flecked eye shadow, a cotton frock with a low-cut neckline, and thrown over her shoulders a coat of black fur fabric. She was rolling a ball of red paper towards the baby girl, and the baby girl was laughing and grabbing it out of her hands. On the sofa against the back wall was a half naked boy. He wore only jeans, and he lay with his hands behind his head and his face in profile to the woman from the Welfare. The girl at least looked at her. She raised the tinselled eyes in one long insolent stare—then she went on playing with the baby girl.

'Is this the little girl?' asked the Welfare worker.

'Yes,' said Lola.

'She looks very nice and clean and healthy,' said the woman.

'Yes.'

Lola rose from the floor and picked up Sharon Faylene and hugged her.

'Goodbye, Sharon,' she whispered.

Sharon Faylene was dressed in her best crocheted coat and her blue shoes. She looked from Lola to the social worker. Then she took a handful of Lola's hair and hid her face in it. Lola tucked her on her hip and walked into the bedroom. She came back with a suitcase, which she thrust at the woman from the Welfare.

'There's everything there,' she said; 'dresses, jackets, napkins, and they're all washed and ironed and she's washed and fed. The kid is not going in for neglect, you know.'

This last was an unfortunate remark. The woman from the Welfare had been deciding for some minutes past that she hated this girl who belonged to the big beautiful boy, sprawled silent there beside the window—the sun glittering on his body.

'Don't I know you?' she asked Lola.

'No you don't,' said Lola.

'Haven't I seen you in court?'

Brownie spoke.

'What's it to you?' he asked.

Lola handed Sharon Faylene to the woman from the Welfare.

'I was bagged for a stretch a couple of years ago,' she said. 'Mind you don't turn my little mate into a vagrant.'

'Are you working now?' asked the woman from the Welfare.

'Listen, don't talk to me like you were a plain-clothes cop.'

Brownie turned and looked at the woman.

'I'm keeping her,' he said. 'Any more questions? No. Well, get going.'

The woman from the Welfare went away with Sharon Faylene in her arms and Sharon Faylene seemed quite contented. All the way down the garden path she waved and blew kisses to Lola.

'She'll like the ride in the car,' said Lola, and then she started to cry. Lola always wept very silently with the mascara running down her cheeks.

They were standing outside the gate—Lola, Brownie and Lyle. It was the day after Sharon Faylene's departure. Mavis had been buried in the morning. Now there were just the three of them, and Lyle was going away. He was standing now astride his bike, hands grasping the handlebars, knapsack strapped on his back. Straight after the funeral he had come home and packed the knapsack. Lola had looked at him across the grave and seen that he was no longer in tears. For the first time in three days he was calm. He wiped his eyes as the earth thudded in, filling the grave, and when the Minister (Church of England—they had dim recollections of Mavis having said once or twice that she had been christened Church of England) told them it was time to leave, he went without any backward glance or seeming distress. He had been very silent on the way home, and as soon as they arrived he had gone into the bedroom and they heard him moving around. Lola, making coffee and sandwiches in the kitchen, listened from time to time, but she heard no further grief. At last he came out with the knapsack on his back, wheeled his bike from underneath the house and told Lola and Brownie:

'I'm going.'

'At least take ten minutes to have some coffee,' cried Lola.

So he did. He drank three cups of coffee and ate two rolls with salami sausage and mustard, and Lola packed him some cheese sandwiches and bananas to eat on the road.

'Where are you going?' she asked.

'First I'm off to Mount Isa. I fixed up about a job there yesterday while I was out when the woman came for Sharon. When I've made enough money I'll move on. I'll see the world if I do nothing else. It's what I always wanted to do.'

So now they were bidding him goodbye before he set off to see the world. Lola looked intently at him. His face was exhausted now of every emotion, drained even of grief, and now Lola felt that, in some way she could not understand, he was relieved. His love was dead. He would never love again. The terrible burden of love lifted from his shoulders for ever, he looked up at the distant hills.

'Well,' he said, 'this is it.' And then. 'I'll never marry again.'

Both Lola and Brownie felt uncomfortable. There was no answer to make. So Lola said:

'I don't think you ever will either.'

'I couldn't,' Lyle still looked away towards the hills as he spoke. 'I couldn't live through it ever again. And I couldn't feel that near to anyone again.'

He shook hands with Brownie, and Lola impulsively threw her arms round him and hugged him.

'We'll go and see Sharo when they let us,' she said.

'Sure, Sharo'll be all right. They look after them well in those places—well, goodbye.'

'Goodbye, God bless you. Write some time.'

'Sure, I'll drop a line.'

'Take care of yourself.'

'Same with you two.'

'Best of luck.'

'Good luck to you.'

'Goodbye.'

'Goodbye.'

Brownie and Lola ran beside the bike a little way, shouting their farewells; then it turned the corner, and as it did so Lyle raised his hand once and looked back at them.

'And that,' said Lola, 'is the last time he'll ever look back in his life.'

She and Brownie entered the garden of No. 20 and it was very still: no radio, no sound of Mavis singing, no tinkling of the bells on Sharon's slippers. The bamboo whispered in the wind, and underneath the house a tap gurgled, stopped and gurgled, regular, maddening, solitary. Lola looked at the sky.

'It only needs the crows to start now,' she said, and suddenly she was clinging to Brownie, trying hard not to become hysterical, but crying on a note of rising terror.

'Thank God you're here, darling; oh, thank God you're here.'

Brownie held her a moment, stroking her shoulders, then he said:

'Go in, get the coffee-pot on, we've got a lot of work to do. Packing and the rest. We're moving out of here this afternoon. We'll stay at a pub or something tonight, and tomorrow I'll pay off and we'll light out for Sydney.'

Quickly they dismantled the bed and stacked it back in the shed with a few other bits of furniture. They packed their clothes and sold the mattresses to the Bottle-oh who made his weekly round that afternoon. They had a final cup of coffee, raked out the fire, piled their cases in a cab and they were gone.

Night-time found the house empty of all save the possums, who came scurrying back from amongst the rafters and the shadow-filled trees. Lola had left the little animals some biscuits, some sugar and some peanut butter, and when they had eaten there was nothing left of human love in the empty rooms—nothing save a ball of red paper thrown in one corner and Mavis's film stars, smiling on the walls.

One morning when he was twenty-one Brownie dressed himself in his new suit (his only suit) and set off to get married. For support he had his old friend the bosun of the *Dalton* who, as he helped him dress, saw fit to reminisce thus:

'Well, Brownie boy, I've had three marriages—all of them spectacular flops. The first cost me fifty quid and maintenance for the kid paid every month right on the knocker till he was sixteen. The second cost me £75 with costs, and two hundred quid in a lump sum. It's going to cost me £500 to get rid of this last bitch, and worth every penny of it every time, me boy. Here's your grey tie, son— trust the old Mad Mariner to think of everything.'

'Gee, I'm nervous,' said Brownie, trying hard to knot the grey tie.

148

'So you well may be, old son.' The Mad Mariner took the tie and made a beautiful job of it. 'There you are, nothing to it. It's the first time hurts the most.'

Brownie laughed.

'Lovely old best man you turned out to be.'

'Ah, don't take any notice of me, Brown, I'm just a sentimental old fool.'

Brownie felt he was bursting with love, delight and confidence. Of course, he had experienced a feeling of misgiving that he could not explain. It was when they first arrived in Sydney and his twenty-first birthday was drawing near. He had always planned to marry the day he turned twenty-one. It had been a day-dream of long standing; and then, as it came nearer to being a fact, he was filled suddenly with foreboding. Lola laughed. She said all men had an inborn resistance to marriage.

'It's handed on from father to son,' she assured him.

'It's just the knowledge that, once married, you can never get away from the little dears without a hell of a lot of unpleasantness and expense,' said the Mad Mariner.

'It's not that at all,' Brownie struggled between amusement, chagrin and inarticulateness. 'It's just that—that, oh well, I don't know, it all seems so awful.'

'Well,' Lola tormented him, 'you've been nagging at me for years to make an honest lad out of you. Now it looks like you want to back out. O.K., we'll forget about it.'

The thought that Lola might not want to tie him down so terrified Brownie that he leaped to the bait.

'It's just—well, you know I'll never leave you. Why do I have to make promises as though I was the sort of dead bastard no girl could trust. Haven't we always been perfectly all right the way we are?'

This conversation took place about a fortnight before the wedding. The Mad Mariner was visiting them, and they all sat on the balcony of the flat they had taken on the Cross. It was not an expensive flat as King's Cross goes, being old, inconvenient and not self-contained, but it had one of the best views in Sydney. The land fell away steeply beneath the balcony so that Elizabeth Bay seemed almost beneath their feet. They sat now watching the spangle of lights grow across the darkening water and finishing off one of Lola's extraordinary meals—lamb chops, because she liked them, spring rolls, because the bosun brought them, fried rice with cabbage because it was her speciality. Now, as she called from the kitchenette behind them, 'Is it coffee or beer for you, boys?' Brownie repeated, 'What's wrong with all this, aren't we perfectly happy the way we are?'

Lola did not answer from the kitchen. They could hear her moving around lighting the gas, rattling cups; and then she switched off the light, and in the darkness the lovely smell of brewing coffee crept to them and mingled with the perfume of the oleander, heavy with blossoms beneath the balcony, and the Florida water that Lola always rubbed in her hair. She came across the balcony to Brownie and put her hands on his shoulders and kissed him.

'You unspeakable cad,' she said with infinite love.

And now it was the wedding morning. All doubts of the future had been banished by the joyous bustle of the last week or so.

150

'I never knew there was so much jazz attached to getting married,' Brownie confessed.

First Brownie had to be hauled off to a Roman Catholic priest, where he was instructed in the principal points of the Catholic faith.

'No priest will marry us without,' explained Lola.

Brownie said that was O.K. He consigned his dreams of a quiet little registry office ceremony to the realm of things best not thought of, or even spoken of if it came to that. Lola, it seemed, had never thought of marriage without the full trimmings, and as she danced around, abrim with excitement, she frequently exclaimed:

'Gee, Brownie! Am I going to be respectable—the young matron, that's me from this on.'

So Brownie went off to learn about the Infallibility of the Pope and went shopping for a new suit and kept to himself his fears that he might die of nerves and stage-fright when the great day came.

And then it was the wedding eve, and Lola's mother was stepping off the plane from Brisbane, stone-cold sober, in a faultless black costume with a rich and mysterious wedding present tucked under the arm. And she and Lola fell upon each other's necks, all smiles and tears and endearments, which left Brownie to marvel much at the ways of women.

Then Brownie was thrown out of the flat for the night, which left him to marvel more, and particularly at Lola's explanation.

'It wouldn't be the right thing, darling. Wouldn't be the right thing at all—as well as being terribly unlucky.'

Then Lola was going to Confession, and he was in the back of the church waiting for her—gazing up at a monstrous statue of Michael the Archangel, and torturing himself with the fantasy that the priest might order six months' celibacy for a penance. However, she came out of the confessional a trifle pink around the ears, but happy, and professing herself to be much relieved in mind. She hauled Brownie off to buy her a cup of coffee, which they had in a little dark espresso down in McLeay Street, and they held hands silently for a long time, like very new lovers indeed. After which they were kissing goodbye outside the flat, and Brownie was holding her with his heart filled with fear, but she put his arms away gently and said:

'It will be all right tomorrow, darling. You'll see. Don't be frightened, Brownie. Wait and see. Tomorrow we're going to marry and live happily ever after.'

Brownie went round to take a room at the hotel where the Mad Mariner was staying, and the Mad Mariner suggested a night on the town as the only cure for his woeful condition. Brownie professed himself aghast at the idea, so the Mad Mariner, like the true and unselfish friend he was, refrained from all references to high-minded young bridegrooms and contented himself with plying his suffering friend with night-caps of whisky and milk (taken hot—another great remedy of the bosun's dear old mother back in Limehouse), till at last Brownie turned in, claiming that he was not going to sleep a wink.

The faithful bosun aroused him at half past nine. Brownie swallowed some coffee and got his eyes open properly in the shower. Then came the dressing. The big ritual was on.

And now they were dressed and speeding through the Cross in a taxi; or, more precisely, they were crawling through a near traffic jam and the cab-driver was leaning out every other yard to abuse mugs in Holdens, dills in Station Wagons, bastards in panel vans, etc. But Brownie had the sensation they were speeding in a golden cloud, and then, alternately, that they were crawling to their doom in a tumbril while hostile crowds shouted:

'There he is, that's the victim! That's the victim!'

Then here they were at Saint Canice's, and the priest was meeting them and shaking them by the hand making gentle little jokes about brides being late, which Brownie could not hear for the roaring in his ears. They waited in the vestry.

'Lucky for you it's a mixed marriage,' said the knowledgeable bosun, 'or you'd be waiting right out there in the big church, stranded all alone there right in front of the altar, feeling a proper guy.'

'She's gone, she's gone,' cried Brownie within himself. 'She's gone. I'll cut my throat. She's late. God, I could belt the daylights out of her.'

There she was getting out of a taxi. She was beautiful, glorious, terrible with banners, in her beautiful, secret wedding clothes. Brownie felt an almost over-whelming urge to rush forward and grovel at her feet in sheer relief. She wore a sheath of golden satin, and a wide white hat, and below it her hair was coiled in an enormous knot on the nape of her neck. Her heels were the highest that could be

153

bought, and her gloves reached to her elbows and fastened with little gilded buttons. She was white and gold from head to toe, and in her hands she carried frangipani and fern.

'Of course, darling,' she had said, 'I can't go as a bride, but I can be smart. So elegance is the keynote, sweetheart. No good striving for that virginal effect.'

She was dazzling, but had she perhaps neglected the virginal look too completely? However, Brownie noticed she had left off her gypsy earrings, and that the split in the back of the sheath skirt was what might be termed, for Lola, discreet. He decided they looked right enough for the Cross. He had a momentary qualm about his own brand new, American-style suit. It had seemed so glorious at the tailor's, and now—he grinned to himself.

'What the hell!' he thought. 'I look like a sailor who's marrying the woman he's been living with for years.'

The Mad Mariner had arranged himself in a sort of modified Ivy League outfit. The effect sought was one of quiet good dressing, the effect achieved was that the Mad Mariner looked like a commercial traveller in one of the less reputable contraceptives. Lola's mother, however, lent the necessary air of respectability. She stood there in the beautifully cut costume and a plain linen blouse. She wore English shoes, very little make-up and no jewellery. Lola had insisted on having a few friends along.

'I'm damned if I'm going to sneak off and marry with only two witnesses,' she had said. 'I don't care what I've done.'

So the landlady came along, and the landlady's daughter, and Joey the landlady's daughter's fiancé, and they were all crowding in behind Lola and Brownie; and now the priest was putting his stole around his neck, and the marriage service had begun, and Brownie was precipitated into vast chasms of stage-fright where coherent thought was no longer possible. For some few moments he had a bewildering mental image as of the vestry filling up with those whose lives had gone to make his and Lola's—his grandmother, Martha Hansen, who would have been near to a stroke had she seen him married by a Catholic priest, his grandfather Hansen who would not have cared where he married, his father of the golden hair and blue eyes, gone no one knew where; and Lola's Irish grandparents and wandering father and Indian great-grandmother, all were there—thronging and whispering shadows around him.

Lola's mother was weeping; the tears were pouring down her face. The landlady was crying. Brownie saw, with a flash of horror, that the Mad Mariner himself was noticeably watery eyed, blew his nose like a bugle, and was so shaken out of his usual aplomb that he dropped the ring right at the priest's feet. Even Brownie, the agnostic, was profoundly moved by the beauty of the ritual. As he promised to love and to cherish, for richer and for poorer, for better and for worse, in sickness and in health, till death, he felt a lump rise in his throat. But Lola! Lola was transformed. She stood, head erect, shoulders thrown back, her eyes tilted with triumph, a faint smile on her mouth, flowers filling her hands, and she made the responses without hesitation, in a clear, ringing voice—Lola radiant, Lola in her glory, Lola the most honest honest-woman in Sydney.

Outside the church, of course, the kissing commenced. Mrs. Lovell kissed Brownie, and said:

'I'm very pleased with my son-in-law.'

Everyone kissed Lola, first and foremost being the Mad Mariner.

'An old friend's privilege, my dear.'

Then Lola tossed her bridal bouquet into the air, and it was caught by a little girl who always stood at the gate taking in all the Saturday morning weddings.

'You'll be next, sweetheart,' teased Lola, and the little girl, who hoped to marry Elvis Presley, remembered this years later when she married a sailor in that self-same church.

Now the Mad Mariner was wringing Brownie by the hand and saying:

'Take care of her, Brown my boy.'

Which caused Brownie to burst out laughing, and the Mad Mariner dropped the straightforward manly tones and returned to normal and said:

'Now be my guest everyone. We'll nip up into the "Mayfair" and drink to the happy couple.'

It was ten o'clock the same night. The wedding reception was going apace—drinks in the bed-sit, food in the kitchen, dancing on the balcony, the last thanks to the taxi-driver from the next flat who had loaned his radiogram and records, brought his girl friend and joined the festivities. Everything was going well. Joey and the landlady's daughter had not yet had the fight with which they always enlivened parties. The Mad Mariner had so far successfully been prevented from making a speech that started: 'I knew these two dear young people when they were living in a cabin aboard the old *Dalton*.'

Lola's mother had delighted all who knew her by having one decorous sip of champagne and refusing hard liquor for the rest of the evening, and she and the Mad Mariner had just performed a Charleston that was considered a great triumph by one and all. Said the Mad Mariner:

'Didn't I say, Brownie boy, that I'd dance at your wedding when you and Lola were down in Melbourne—'

'Have a drink bosun,' said Brownie, wondering if there were any precedent for doping the best man's grog.

Lola was standing by herself at the edge of the balcony, looking down at Elizabeth Bay. She was, for a moment, isolated in one of those little seas of silence that can close around one at a party. She was very happy and very tired. She had been up early; she had spent all the afternoon cleaning the flat, helping with the savouries and so on, and she had been rocking and rolling almost non-stop for a couple of hours. She bent down and pulled off the lovely wedding shoes. She felt the cool of the tesselated floor strike through her stockings, and she sighed blissfully.

Brownie came up to her and put his hand on her arm.

'Let's shoot through for a while,' he said.

'Where to?'

'Anywhere—just to be alone together on our wedding day. Get into something comfortable and we'll blow.'

Lola looked down at the crumpled golden sheath with love.

'Oh, Brownie,' she said, 'I couldn't take this off. I want to be buried in it.'

157

Brownie laughed. 'O.K., but let's go.'

So Lola slipped into comfortable scuffs and put Brownie's duffle jacket across her shoulders and they went into the kitchen and told Mrs. Lovell they were going. She nodded.

'A good idea,' she said. 'I'll handle this crowd here.'

Once in the street they caught a taxi and then had no idea where they wanted to go.

'I'll run you down to the ferry and you can go across to Manly,' said the taxi-driver. 'That's where all the lovers go, isn't it, eh?'

He turned around and smiled at them.

'Lovers!' scoffed Lola. 'We're an old married couple.'

The taxi-driver's smile broadened.

'Lady,' he said, 'wipe the confetti out of your eyelashes.'

So they went to Manly where all the lovers go, but it was a little early in the season for lovers, and they strolled along in the darkness all alone, the way Brownie wanted it. They sat beneath the pine trees and looked out at the immensity of the Pacific, black that night because there was no moon, black with lines of white where the surf rolled shorewards. Lola turned round so that she could lean against Brownie and stretch her legs along the rest of the seat. He put his arms around her and drew her closer to him. She was silent for a while and then she said:

'You know what, Brownie, we've got responsibilities now and, just think, you're twenty-one, I'm nearly twenty.'

'Well, I hadn't noticed any actual senile decay.'

'No, but no longer do we have the old teen-ager excuse.'

'I was a teen-age werewolf.'

'I just mean no one is going to feel sentimental about us any more.'

'I never noticed anyone ever did.'

'No, but we were a fashionable section of society and now we're not. We're old married squares.'

Brownie kissed the top of her head.

'Feels good doesn't it?' he said.

'You ridiculous boy, I'm trying to be serious.'

'The young matron, of course.'

'Yes, I am, and what I'm saying is we're married, responsible people. You might be a father by this time next year. How do you feel about that? Scared, eh?'

'No, of course not.'

'Darling Brownie, you're never scared.'

Brownie rose to his feet and took her by the hand. Together they walked to where the edge of the surf hissed up along the sand. Far across the water, making for North Head, the lights of a steamer shone through the dark. They stood without speaking for a moment then Lola linked her arm through Brownie's.

'Oh, darling,' she said, 'it's terrible to end this day. Why must we get tired? But I am tired, sweetheart, so take me home to bed.'

Brownie nodded.

'Yes,' he said. 'I'll take you home.'

And still looking out at the ship that glowed in the night he took a two-shilling piece from his pocket and flung it far into the surf.

'The sea buys your gear,' he said, 'and the sea and I are going to look after you until the day I die.'

159

Text Classics